CARIBBEAN RESCUE

Billionaire Beach Romance

CAMI CHECKETTS

Birch River Publishing

COPYRIGHT

DEDICATION

It's interesting to write a book with two deadbeat fathers when I had the most amazing dad that I know. Thank you, Dad, for making everything fun and always being there for me. You are the most patient person I know, and I'll be forever grateful for all the times you demonstrated that patience. I can't believe I blew up your truck motor, and you never even raised your voice. I love you.

FREE BILLIONAIRE BRIDE PACT ROMANCE

Sign up for Cami's newsletter and receive a free ebook copy of *The Feisty One: A Billionaire Bride Pact Romance* here.

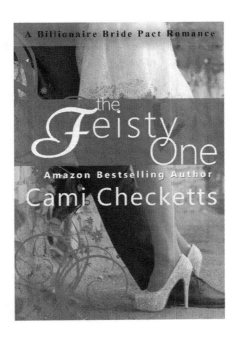

CHAPTER ONE

Madeline Panetto rushed down the lower hallway of the yacht, praying she wouldn't run into one of her father's men. A hand snaked around her arm and pulled her to a stop. Madeline swung a fist and connected with a muscular shoulder. The man grunted and yanked her against his chest.

"Don't worry, la mia bella donna." Bello breathed into her neck. Maddie cringed, wanting to punch him again. "It is only me."

He was exactly who she'd been hoping to avoid. Bello made her skin crawl with his insinuations that she should be into him. Where was her father when she needed him? Bello had been quick to tell Maddie that his name meant handsome in Italian as he gave her a leering wink. During the past week and a half, she'd worked hard to avoid his wandering hands and suggestive looks, but it was a full-time job. He was handsome, tall, and dark, but his soul was twisted and ugly. She'd figured out his true character within her first five minutes on the yacht and changed his name to Bello the Butthole. It had a nice rhythm, and it completely fit.

"I need to get dressed for dinner." Maddie succeeded in pulling her arm free.

"I could help you change." Bello winked and trailed his fingers along her collarbone.

Maddie shivered and backed up a step. "I'm a big girl; I think I can handle it."

"You are a big girl." His eyes slithered over her body.

Yuck. Maddie felt like she'd been dunked in a tub of manure.

"You know, every time we ... stop a boat ..." He cleared his throat and grinned like they were sharing some secret, like she didn't know what kind of a vicious and despicable scumball he was. "The women beg for me to take care of them. I think you'll find you enjoy the experience."

Maddie barely stopped herself from slapping him. Hands trembling with rage at what those poor women had gone through—what she might go through if she didn't get off this ship—she scurried around him and ran down the hallway. Tripping on nothing, she righted herself quickly and kept moving.

"See you at dinner. I hope you're wearing something special for me."

"I hope you burn in purgatory!" Maddie screamed back, hating the smirk on his lips and knowing look in his eyes. He was going to force himself on her if she wasn't very, very careful.

Her heart rate didn't return to normal even after she reached her own room and locked the door. Dressing quickly with trembling fingers, she secured the heavy diamond necklace around her throat; a graduation gift from her father. She wished she could avoid facing Bello at dinner, but she'd be safe if she stayed close to her father. Bello acted like a gentleman when his boss was within ear's length.

She checked her reflection, liking the floor-length, teal-colored lace dress. Teal worked with her dark hair and olive skin. She supposed she was a good combination of her Italian father and Spanish mother, but hoped she was nothing like them in moral structure. Maybe it was wrong to blame her mother for lying to her for twenty-four years. She had been a decent single parent and a good example of a hardworking, well-educated woman, but the lying ... It made Maddie want to disown both her parents.

The luxurious Sussurro Yacht swayed slightly, but she'd gotten used to that after a few days. If only she could get used to being around her father and the awful men he called friends, business associates, pirate mates, mafia connections. Which name fit?

Maddie shuddered. Her father was a pirate. *Didn't see that one coming.* She'd never thought of herself as thick-headed, but obviously she must have been not to have realized who or what her father was and then agree to sail around the Caribbean with him as a graduation present. Oh, to go back to the simplicity of college life. Her master's thesis had been much easier than this ploy of a trip. Faking that she was comfortable around Bello the Butthole made her want to wear baggy sweats to dinner and pretend she was deaf. But that wasn't possible. Instead, she'd have to dress appropriately in her diamond necklace and Bergdorf Goodman evening gown—which was ridiculous, considering the price tag was probably over seven grand.

Loud bangs and thumps came from above. Maddie jerked and glanced at the ceiling as if it had the answer to the sudden disturbance. A gunshot rang out. Maddie ducked instinctively. Terror pricked at her spine as her hands grew clammy and her body trembled.

Where could she go to be safe? They'd look in the closet, and the bed frame was attached to the floor. Could she jump overboard and hope she could make it to one of the many Caribbean islands? Oh, man! She'd been ticked at her father off and on throughout her life, usually because she wanted his attention and he wasn't around, but at this moment, she truly hated him. Maybe she'd get lucky and her father's employees would shoot each other and leave her alone. Maybe this was just another idiotic way these men passed the time. The only reason they hadn't used her to pass the time was that her father would've slit their throats. *Piece of dung pirates.*

Maddie grabbed a heavy picture frame off the table and crept toward the door. She wasn't going to sit here and wait for somebody to come kill her. The walkie-talkie her father had given her to communicate onboard the ship buzzed as more shots and some loud thumps came from above. "Madeline," her father panted out. "Meet me at my room. Now."

"Is everything—" she started, but he'd clicked off.

Maddie clung to the walkie-talkie and the picture frame and slowly opened her door. There was no sound in the hallway. Hopefully all the action was upstairs, and she could make it down the passageway to her father's room without being shot.

Another gun discharged, and she jumped and screamed. *Forget caution.* She sprinted down the hall—not an easy feat in a tight evening gown. A rip of fabric informed her she'd damaged the dress. The only reason she cared was that she'd hoped to resell the gowns to fund some humanitarian trips.

She banged through the door and into the suite at the rear of the boat. This yacht was massive. She'd never seen anything like it except on those television specials where they toured ridiculously wealthy people's homes and yachts.

Thankfully, her father's room was quiet and dark. She didn't dare flip on the lights, but called out softly, "Papa?" It wasn't a term of endearment anymore, just what he'd expected her to call him during his infrequent visits. She'd taken to calling him *father* the past few years to tick him off, but in her terror, the old term came out.

No answer.

Maddie shut the door behind her and turned on a side lamp, not wanting the bright overhead light on. She set her picture frame down and crept toward his safe. He'd told her the combination when he gave her a tour of the ship and told her to take out the weapons, money, papers sealed in a waterproof packet, and the flash drive if there was ever an emergency.

She wondered if they'd been attacked by another pirate ship; apparently there were a whole slew of them. Maybe his troops had started an uprising. Her father controlled them with an iron fist, and the fear in his staff's eyes made her sick. Maybe they were finished being afraid.

Quickly unlocking the safe, she pulled out a pistol first and inserted bullets into the chamber. Her hands only shook slightly. One of the few things her father had taught her when he'd visited—besides the fact he adored her mother, and Maddie was an unfortunate by-product of their romance—was how to shoot a sidearm.

The door cracked open. Maddie whirled, her finger tightening on the trigger.

"It's me," her father, Armando, whispered, sliding into the room.

"Nice job getting the revolver." He slid the deadbolt to secure the door, then pushed a heavy dresser in front of it.

Maddie's arm slackened to her side as she watched him. Finally, she found her voice. "What's going on?"

"Bello has made his play."

"I thought you trusted him. You said he was like a son to you." Her voice escalated with her terror.

"Lesson learned. Never trust anyone, my love."

He had no right to use terms of endearment. "What does he want?"

"My money. My power." He shook his head and strode past her to the safe, muttering, "And you."

Maddie's entire body shuddered. She'd rather be ripped apart by a shark; at least she could retain her virtue and self-respect. "And you're just going to barricade us in here and hope he changes his mind? Great plan, Pops."

"I've got a better one." He pulled the flash drive that was sealed in plastic out of the safe and handed it to her. "This is the most important thing I will ever give you. Keep it safe until you can turn it over to Homeland Security. Hide it where you won't lose it."

Maddie tucked it into her bra.

"Good girl." He entered a code and then yanked open a side door. Maddie found herself looking at a small boat. "Get in. Bello and I had planned to have you take the papers and flash drive to America when we dropped you off in San Juan next week and make us honest men, but apparently he has other plans. At least he doesn't know about the escape boat. It's nothing fancy, but should get you to the nearest island. Go west or south." He actually smiled like this was funny.

Maddie's stomach dropped. How was she supposed to know what direction to go in the dark? "Me or us?"

"Only you. I'll hold them off as long as I can." Her father shoved the sealed bag into her hands. "This is a paper copy of everything on the drive, some cash, and several different passports, social security cards, and birth certificates for you and your mother."

"What? Reverse a minute. Go back to why you aren't coming with me." She didn't like her father, but she didn't want Bello killing him, and she really, really didn't want to be alone on the ocean at night.

Her father grasped her upper arms in his thick hands. He was a strong man and had probably been good-looking before a life of thieving, lying, and too much alcohol robbed him of his youth and his daughter's respect. "I'm dying."

Maddie's mouth opened, but no words came out.

"It's all right, love. The liver's gone. Cirrhosis. I'll be glad to be done with all of this." He gestured toward the door and the gunshots. "I'll miss seeing your mother ..." His eyes glossed over for a second before he focused in on her again. "And I'll miss you."

Maddie knew that was a lie. Though he took her mother on extravagant vacations several times a year, he rarely came to see Maddie, and this was the first time she'd been invited to go anywhere with him. It was turning out fabulous.

"But I've made my peace with God and man, and I'll die protecting my beautiful daughter."

Maddie had to bite her tongue, not sure how a pirate who fed off others' fears and misfortunes could make peace with anyone on heaven or earth. A banging on the door and a barrage of bullets into it announced Bello and his cronies. Maddie jumped but luckily didn't scream this time.

"The drive will explain everything, and it also has access to accounts that will make you a wealthy woman. Hold on to the papers if at all possible, but the drive is essential." He bent down and kissed her forehead then gave her a brief hug. "You're the best part of me, my love. Thank you for becoming so much better than I could've dreamed." He directed her into the boat and sat her down. It wasn't much bigger than a canoe, but it had a motor at the back. "When you get to land, follow the instructions. Someone I trust will come pick you up and help you create a new life and identity. Your mother too."

"But I just graduated." Six years of hard work down the crapper because of her father. If he wasn't dying, she'd be tempted to shoot him.

He smiled that placating smile parents gave to two-year-olds. "You can pick whatever degree you want. Don't go to Belize, Honduras, or Grand Cayman. Bello and the other pirate captains won't stop looking for you until the Coast Guard uses that information to capture them.

America should be safe. They'll be more leery of the U.S. authorities." He nodded to her. "Be safe and be happy, my love."

Another barrage of bullets came at the door. Maddie's heart was in her throat. She had no clue how to say goodbye to a father who had caused her to doubt her worth her entire life. Yet she didn't want him to die from cirrhosis or Bello's gun. This was the first time in her life that he'd seemed to care, and now he would die protecting her from Bello.

Her father pushed a button, and before Maddie had time to say anything, the boat was lowered into the water. She clung to the sealed packet and the gun, watching her father's face.

"Start the motor," he yelled. "There's a pull cord at the back. Go." The ropes released her boat, and it almost capsized from the force of the yacht's wake. Maddie bit her lip to keep from crying out.

The compartment closed and the yacht sped off, her little boat bobbing in the waves. She held on to the side and prayed. Maddie could see men on deck with guns drawn. Luckily, it was a dark night and they didn't notice her. Soon the yacht was pinpricks of lights in the distance.

Maddie shuddered, set the packet and pistol underneath a seat, and turned to figure out how to start the motor. It wasn't cold, but her fingers felt like ice as she fumbled in the dark for switches and a pull cord. The boat reminded her of something she'd seen old men fishing in, a simple design with the motor and handle at the back that was used for steering.

"All the money in the world and this is his escape plan," she muttered. "If I built a secret compartment in a yacht, I would've put a James Bond boat in it, or something rocking cool. You're pathetic!" she yelled at her father. Too much distance and noise separated them for him to hear her. He'd never hear her again. A tear traced down her face, and she brushed it angrily away.

Tugging several times on the cord that would hopefully start the motor yielded nothing. She pulled out something she thought was a choke lever and yanked the pull cord again. The motor sounded but sputtered out after a few seconds. Maddie's cry of joy turned quickly to despair. She sat there for a few seconds, watching where the yacht had disappeared. When they discovered she was gone, would they come for her? Had they already ... killed her father? Another fat tear slid down her cheek, frustrating her. Ironic that all she'd wanted an hour ago was to disappear to any deserted island rather than spend another minute around her father and Bello. She should be more careful what she wished for.

She yanked on the motor cord again. It sprang to life but sputtered out. What was she forgetting? The choke thing had helped her start it, but was it just for starting?

Water splashed against the boat, and she could've sworn something smacked the side. She glanced around nervously, but it was too dark to see anything. Sharks? Eels? She had to get out of here.

Maddie's hands were slick with sweat as she pulled the starter one more time and then quickly pushed the choke lever forward. The motor stayed alive. *Yes!* She fumbled around with other levers until she must've put it into gear, because the boat sprang forward. Directing the rudder on the motor, she aimed away from where the yacht had gone and started praying. *Help me find land and someone nice who will help me.* She wasn't sure that she trusted anyone her father had arranged to get her to safety and set up a new identity. Why should she change her whole life because of her father or Bello? Maybe she could just appeal to Homeland Security, the FBI, or whatever governmental department dealt with pirates. They could catch Bello and the other pirate captains, and then she'd be safe. First, she needed to get through this huge ocean and find some help.

The wind started picking up, and Maddie's terror increased right along with it. The Caribbean was generally calmer than the Pacific or the Atlantic, but storms could come through and cover entire islands with waves. Her little boat wouldn't have a prayer in a real storm. *Please keep me safe. Please let the storm calm down.*

Her prayers didn't seem to be working. The wind whipped her hair out of its updo and tugged at the delicate lace overlay of her dress. Water splashed over the sides of the boat. She went up and down, wave after wave. The little boat barely stayed afloat, not seeming to make any progress.

She fumbled around with her left hand, but couldn't find a life jacket. Her dress clinging to her, Maddie shook from cold and wet as much as from fear. Everything around her was dark, and she wondered if she should have stayed on the yacht and taken her chances with Bello and his henchmen. No. Drowning was preferable to being in Bello's clutches without her father around to protect her. *Her father*. She could only imagine what Bello would do to him. What a horrible way to die.

A huge wave rocked her boat and soaked her clear through. Her heart clutched before picking up to staccato speed. She was going to die. This was it. She'd see her dad up in heaven a lot sooner than she'd planned. Well, maybe not. He definitely wasn't going to heaven, and she might've ruined her chances this past week when she'd regularly cursed all those men behind their backs. A valiant missionary she was not.

Maddie squinted through the darkness, searching, praying. She saw nothing. The water in the boat was up to her ankles. The little motor kept chugging along, but it seemed to be going slower. *Please, a little help*, she begged. She'd always communed with the good Lord, but never quite so frequently.

She wondered if she should stop and scoop water out of the boat, but then she'd have to release her hold on the lever directing her, and the boat might just spin in circles. She shoved heavy, wet hair from her face. Not that she knew what direction she was going in now. She instinctively reached for her cell phone, but it sat on her nightstand in the yacht. Since she didn't have an international plan, she'd stopped carrying it everywhere with her, but she could've at least used it as a compass.

Rain started pelting her from above as the waves splashed over her boat and hit her from below. "Really?" She tossed the words to the sky. "Hasn't my life been hard enough? Now I have to die in complete misery."

Truthfully, her life hadn't been too awful. Her mom was a professor at Montana State University, and they'd had a good life together in the small, beautiful mountain valley, loved and helped by friends and church members. Things only looked down when her father stole her mother away on some exotic vacation and left Maddie behind at her friend Abby's. Not that she didn't enjoy being with Abby, but she'd always dreamed of going with them on their trips. Now she'd finally gotten a taste of one of those vacations, and she couldn't believe her competent, smart mother had never divorced the louse.

Both her parents had lied to her throughout her life. "Papa's away on important business," her mother would always say. Ridiculous.

"Focus," Maddie muttered to herself. Blaming her parents wouldn't get her out of this predicament.

She scanned the darkness, praying, hoping. Blinking twice, she couldn't be sure if she'd really seen some lights, or if she was just getting delusional and desperate. But no ... or actually, yes. Yes! There were some dots of light to her left. She jerked the handle too hard in her excitement and almost capsized the boat. Yelping, she straightened it out and tried again more slowly.

A tingle of uncertainty lurked in her mind. What if it was the pirates coming back for her? But she really had no hope but to try for the lights. If it started to look like a ship, she'd change course. A full-size cruise ship would take her boat under, and a yacht had too much risk of being Bello.

As she slowly drew closer, she squinted to make out the shape of whatever she was approaching. The arrangement of lights looked too spread out to be a ship. It had to be an island. Letting out a squeal of joy, she leaned forward as if she could help the little boat go faster.

The island grew larger on the horizon. She could see lights down by the beach, and a cluster of windows were lit up on the hill. Details came into focus. It was one huge house—or maybe hotel—on the hilltop, and there was an inlet/harbor kind of thing. She could just make out the outline of a yacht in the harbor. There were some tiki torches on the beach a couple hundred yards away from the harbor and a fabulous long dock, stretching out into the ocean.

All she had to do was make it to the dock. She might crash into it due to her lack of boating skills, but she could grab the packet and swim for it if she had to. Hopefully, someone in that house or hotel would be trustworthy and willing to help. *Pathetic that she'd rather take her chances with strangers than trust her dad's people.* Not that her dad had ever put her in serious danger before.

Wait, that's all this trip had been: danger. Why had he brought her here now? Just to tell her he was dying, say goodbye, and have her clear his name? Couldn't he have done that without yucky Bello around?

Maddie saw movement on the long dock. A large man was waving his arms and yelling at her, but she couldn't make out his words.

The boat slammed into something. Maddie had no time to think or react as she flew over the front of the boat and plunged into the water.

CHAPTER TWO

Zack Tyndale heard the wind howling and hurried around the sprawling one-story mansion, closing windows and doors. The house had been built to withstand hurricanes, so he knew he'd be safe in a normal storm, but he liked to be prepared. He rushed outside to make sure his small yacht was secure in the harbor and nothing was lying around that would be blown away. Thankfully, the previous owner had been prepared for these gales. Everything from the patio furniture to the grill was secured to the concrete, and all outside tools and toys were stored nicely in the convenient storage containers.

Zack loved his island and the local flair to his mansion. Such a nice break to be here in the usually calm Caribbean after the hell his life had become in America. He missed his mom and his niece, Chalise, but there was no other reason for him to stay and deal with his father and the constant attention for his failed Olympic hopes.

His satellite phone rang, and he smiled. "Hi, Mom."

"Son. It's about time you came back to work."

Zack's body stiffened. So his father was using his mom's phone to try to make his demands now. No way was he going back. The damage had been done, the barriers erected, and he wasn't ready to forgive and forget. "I'm not coming back to work for you. Ever."

"I need you, son, and your mother and Chalise need you. Stop being selfish and come home."

Selfish? His father dared call *him* selfish? "The world doesn't revolve around you, *Dad*." He knew his father would hate that casual term. "I'm happy here. I don't need your money or your company."

"But think of the time you could spend with Chalise."

Of course his father would hit him with the one thing that tore him apart: not being with his niece. "I should have custody of her; you know that's what Anne would want."

A heavy sigh came across the line. "I'll pay you anything to have you here with your family."

It always came back to money. His father wanted him because Zack had proven himself brilliant with business and was able to charm even their toughest associates. He couldn't be the pawn of a man like his father, not even for Chalise. "I'll never work for you again." He hung up the phone and stormed onto the patio.

Zack watched the wind whip through his trees. The solar lights the original owner had set up on the docks and near the beach swayed. The energy of the storm and fury at his father raced through him, making him want to go run for a while. Rain started to splatter onto the pool deck and landscaped flowerbeds and grass. Protected under the large overhang, he stretched for a minute. Maybe he'd go inside and cook or clean something, since he couldn't run. When the weather was bad, it wasn't as easy to keep busy, and being bored meant thinking about what had happened to his life. Thinking wasn't something he liked to do.

A few steps from the French doors, he heard the high whine of a motor. Zack whipped around and searched the ocean beyond. There were no lights, but the motor sound was unmistakable. What kind of an idiot would be out on the water with no lights and in what sounded like a small boat?

Zack raced past his pool and gardens and took the steps to the beach two at a time. He could just make out a small boat hurtling through the water. He didn't even have time to be angry that someone was invading his sanctuary as he saw the angle they traveled toward the island. "No, not that way!" he yelled, though they couldn't possibly hear him.

Zack sprinted through the sand and onto his dock. He kept one eye on the boat as he ran the length of the dock, waving his arms and yelling, "Turn! Turn!" Large boulders and a former shipwreck resided just under the water, exactly where that boat was heading. Any other angle into the harbor was deep and safe to take even in his yacht, but this idiot was coming straight for the shallow waters of the dock instead. Why weren't they slowing even though they were within a hundred feet of the dock?

"Stop!" he screamed. "Turn!"

The sickening crunch was louder than the howling wind and rain. The rear of the boat flung into the air, and the lone passenger flew forward and disappeared into the water. Zack dove off the dock, surfacing quickly, and used strong strokes to cross the distance. Water from the uneven waves splashed into his face, making it hard to see. The person bobbed up out of the water and started swimming in his direction. That was a relief. From the hair streaming around her, he assumed it was a woman.

They came within a few feet of each other, and Zack slowed and treaded water. "Are you okay?"

"I-I think so."

"Can you make it to the dock?" Lights reflecting from the beach showed a mop of dark hair and a beautiful face.

In answer, she started slowly swimming that direction, but she hadn't gone four strokes before she swayed and rolled over onto her back. That's when Zack noticed the cut on her head. The sea turned the blood a watery pink. She'd definitely hit her head on one of the rocks or maybe the old shipwreck.

"You're not okay."

"I can make it." She started to kick. A wave rolled over her face and she jerked up, coughing and spluttering, but bravely kept trying to stay afloat, beating at the water with her arms and legs.

She was tough and not a complainer. Nice.

"I've got you." Zack looped his arm under her armpit and over her chest and tugged her back to the dock. She had a small build, but her clothes must've been waterlogged because she seemed to weigh a ton. Zack was in shape, but he tired quickly.

Finally, they made it to the dock and the woman clung to the edge. Zack grabbed hold and heaved himself out of the water then helped lift her up. She collapsed onto her back and released a loud breath. "Oh, thank you. I thought it was time to reacquaint myself with Saint Peter."

"Saint Peter?" She'd hit her head hard, or she was crazy. He looked over her fancy, waterlogged dress and the diamonds sparkling at her throat. She'd been out in the ocean like that, without a lifejacket? Crazy it might be or with quite a good story to tell.

"You know—the angel at the pearly gates."

Zack let out a surprised laugh. "Glad you put that off for a little while."

"Me, too." She sat up and touched the small gash in her head. Blood trickled between her fingertips. "Ouch."

"I bet." Zack pushed his way to his feet and offered her a hand. The wind whipped his wet T-shirt around him. He was glad he shaved his head and didn't have hair whipping in his face like she did. "Let's get you up to the house and cleaned up."

She placed her hand in his but wavered as he helped her up. Zack wrapped his other arm around her waist and lifted her onto her feet. She swayed.

"Can you walk?"

Her eyes filled with stubborn pride. "Of course I can walk."

She pulled away from him, took one step, teetered off the dock, and splashed back into the water.

"Oh, boy." Zack shook his head. He hadn't smelled alcohol on her breath, but that had to be the explanation. Fancy dress, alone on a boat in the ocean at night. He'd have to help her tonight, then load her onto his yacht tomorrow and get her to Belize. If she had any money, it was probably sunk with her little boat. He'd get her to where she needed to go and be done with this mess. Oddly enough, he didn't mind the excitement. It was a good contrast to his normally sedate lifestyle.

She came up to the surface sputtering and flailing. Zack knelt down, put his hands under her armpits, and hefted her back onto the dock. He stood slowly, supporting both of them, then swung her off her feet and into his arms. Despite himself, he noticed how nicely she fit against him. It had been a long while since he'd been around an attractive, unrelated woman. "Shall we try this again?"

"Good plan." Her voice rumbled against his chest, and he kind of liked it. "I must've thumped my head harder than I thought."

"Or something," he muttered.

Her head whipped up, her brown eyes full of fire. "I'm not drunk, if that's what you're thinking. I'm ..." She quickly looked down again, not meeting his gaze.

"You're ..." he encouraged. He'd like to hear her story, and he did believe her that she wasn't drunk. Her speech was too lucid and her breath smelled too clean.

"I can't. I don't know who to trust." She grabbed on to his arm. "Oh, holy monkey balls!"

Zack jerked in surprise and almost dropped her as she squirmed in his arms. "What are you doing now? You want to fall in the water again?" They'd reached the end of the dock, but she could still fall in the shallow water.

"I've got to find something. Please. Can you help me look in the water? Back where my boat is?" Her eyes were wide and frantic.

"Right now?" Zack gestured to the waves building as the storm increased in intensity. "No! You're hurt. It's dark. And there's a storm." His four-year-old niece had more common sense than this woman, and Chalise hadn't spoken a word in two years.

The woman deflated and burrowed herself into his arms. Zack liked this quite a bit better than her struggling. He tightened his hold on her. Hmm, her shape was really ... shapely.

"In the morning?" she asked.

"What?"

"Could you help me find something that was in my boat in the morning?"

Zack plunged off the dock and into the sand. He paused to readjust his grip on her. She wrapped her bare arms around his neck and glanced up at him with liquid brown eyes. Those eyes were big and pretty. He'd probably do about anything she asked, pressed against him like she was and arousing feelings he'd denied himself the past two years in his self-induced exile.

"Um, sure. If the storm's gone." The boat and everything in it would probably be pummeled and scattered by the wind and waves.

"Oh, thank you." She tightened her hold on him and cuddled up against his chest.

Zack trudged through the sand and up the stairs. He should've been tired from the effort of the night, but his heart was pumping quickly, and he felt like he could run miles with her cuddled up to him.

They made it to the pool deck, and he set her on her feet by the outside shower, keeping her close to his side. He rinsed off his feet quickly and then hefted her up again.

"I think I can walk now," she protested.

"At least there's no water you can fall into here."

She laughed softly, and he kept her in his arms. He didn't want to let her walk just yet. They reached the patio door, and he had to set her down again. He opened the box of beach towels and handed a couple to her. She wrapped one around her shoulders, then proceeded to try to dry her dress.

"It's okay," Zack said. "The floor's slate. A little water won't hurt it." It would actually be good to get his house a little dirty. He dusted and cleaned, but there wasn't much dirt that accumulated with one person.

He picked her up and carried her through the door and into the great room.

She glanced around and whistled. "I like your house."

"Thanks."

"Are you ... alone?" Her brow wrinkled, and her voice held fear for the first time.

"Yes."

She nodded, but didn't look up at him. Her body stiffened in his arms.

"Hey, you came to me, remember?" Zack tried to tease, but it had a reverse effect. She tried to squirm out of his arms. "Relax. I'm not going to hurt you."

He set her on a barstool in the kitchen. "Let me look at that gash, and then you can shower and get cleaned up."

She pressed her lips into a thin line, her eyes filled with apprehension.

Zack didn't know if it would make any difference, but he tried to reassure her. "I promise I'm not going to hurt you."

She nodded, but from the way she was twisting her hands together, she obviously wasn't comfortable with him.

"What's your name?"

"Maddie," she murmured.

"Short for Madison?" He glanced over her smooth, light brown skin and long dark hair. Even after the trauma she'd just gone through, and with smudges of makeup under her eyes, she was gorgeous. He couldn't imagine how good she'd look all fixed up.

"Madeline."

"Pretty name." Zack wasn't usually so soft, but she was like a scared kitten that would bolt if he didn't set down the milk and step away. Being mostly alone for two years, he hadn't realized he might actually want some company until it landed in his lap. Walking to the medicine cabinet, he found a large Band-Aid and Neosporin, then got a couple of paper towels and moistened them. She was staring up at him with those liquid eyes when he came back. He lifted the paper towels and gently pressed it against her wound. The blood had stopped and clotted. It didn't look deep. Blotting away as much as he could, he was surprised at the charge between them. He wanted to keep staring at her, and he wanted to pick her up in his arms again.

"Thanks." She held his gaze, and as the seconds ticked by, he could feel that her fear of him lessened. But why was she afraid? Had someone hurt her?

"I guess we should wait on the Band-Aid until after you shower."

"Oh. Okay."

"Are you thirsty? Hungry?"

"Water sounds wonderful."

He got a glass of ice water for her and one for himself. They sat there in silence for a few seconds. The water tasted good. He hadn't realized how thirsty he was. Maddie appeared to have finally relaxed around him. Her shoulders were lowered, and she wasn't clenching her hands together.

She glanced down at her dress. "You don't happen to have any clothes my size?" She gave a light laugh.

Zack wished he could return the laugh. "Actually, I do, or at least pretty close."

Her eyes lost the sparkle they'd just gained. "Girlfriend?"

Zack found that amusing. He'd had plenty of girlfriends when he'd been a world-class athlete and well-known heir to a fortune. Now he had none. "No. I have some of my sister's clothes here." Because his mom had been tossing them out, dealing with the loss in her own way. Zack had acted like a sentimental fool and stolen some from the Goodwill bag.

"Will she care if I wear them?"

Zack's lips tightened. "She's dead." He spun around before she could respond or those dark eyes could fill with pity. Then he strode from the room, throwing a glance back over his shoulder. "Stay there. I'll get the clothes and some other stuff for you and put it in the guest room; then I'll come help you."

"Thanks," she called after him.

"Sure." Zack hurried down the hallway as if he could escape the injustice of his only sister, Anne, being ripped from his life. Her husband, Tim, had been killed in the same small plane accident. Tim had been his best friend. Now his niece was an orphan, and Zack was without friends and supporters in his fight against his father. His mom was great, but she had no backbone. Running had been his only option. At least he was a fast runner.

———

Maddie sat exactly where he'd left her, watching his muscled form striding from the open great room. She hadn't even asked his name, but he was obviously an athlete with that tall, lean build. The striations in his calves rocked. Why was he so familiar? The first time she'd glanced up into his handsome face with the chocolate skin and eyes, she'd felt the recognition but couldn't place him. His head was shaved bald, but he didn't need hair to be much too attractive. He was obviously wealthy and alone on this island in this huge house. Maybe he was somebody famous.

The house was unreal. Floor-to-ceiling windows circled the open great room. The kitchen was bright with white cabinets and stainless steel appliances. The red and teal-blue accents wove into the tans and grays of the granite countertop and slate floor and were used in the decorations and throw pillows on the white and tan furniture. It all brought the feeling of comfort and vacation.

Maddie was embarrassed she'd reacted poorly when he admitted they were alone. He wasn't Bello, and he was right—she'd come to him. How crazy all of this was. Two weeks ago, she and her mom had been celebrating her master's degree in the middle of the mountains of Montana. Now she was surrounded by water, her father was most likely dead, and Bello was probably after her. Did she dare trust this guy? How could she not trust him? He was all she had.

She was a mess. And losing that packet of papers ... She groaned. *So dumb.*

She placed her hand over her chest and felt the bulge of the flash drive in her bra. Thank heavens it was in a sealed packet and she hadn't ruined it with her dunking in the ocean. She could ask to use this man's computer and find the information she needed about her father, find out what he wanted her to get to Homeland Security and what fortune he'd left for her. But at this moment she had no money, passports, or number to call. Did her father say the number for help was on the flash drive, too? Would this guy have a satellite phone or something, living out here isolated like this?

It hurt her head to think about it all. She was still dizzy from hitting the rock and trying to swim with this dress on. The guy holding her and carrying her up to his house had been the safest she'd felt since her father had picked her up at the San Juan airport a week and a half ago.

The man walked back into the room. Maddie smiled to try to show him she wasn't scared of him, but the situation felt kind of sticky. He was well built, and they were alone on his island; he could do whatever he wanted to her, and no one would know she'd even been here. No, she couldn't think like that. He'd done nothing but be kind to her. She had so many questions for him. He probably had more for her. Crap. What was she going to tell him? Could she fake amnesia? She had hit her head pretty good.

"What's your name?" she asked.

"Zack."

Maddie stuck out her hand. He shook it with a firm grip and a smile. She liked the contrast of his brown skin and white teeth. She wondered if he had different nationalities in his family line like she did. Maybe African and European? She studied his hands—beautifully formed with long, tapered fingers. "Nice to meet you, Zack. You seem really familiar to me."

He dropped her grip and the smile, eyeing her like she might gouge his eyes out. "Let's get you cleaned up." Swooping her into his arms again, he marched into a hallway also lined with windows.

Obviously he must be someone famous, or he wouldn't have cared that he looked familiar. He'd gotten testy when he'd told her about his sister, too, but she didn't blame him for that. She'd wanted a sibling her whole life and couldn't imagine how hard it would be to have a sibling, then lose her to death.

Maddie found herself relaxing and enjoyed leaning against his muscled chest, which was distinctly displayed by the wet T-shirt. He smelled like salt water and laundry detergent.

They entered a large bedroom with a white four-poster bed and bedroom furniture. The slate floor was covered with a plush rug that was tan, orange, and blue. The bedspread weaved the three colors together nicely. The decorations were nautical and fun *with* huge windows covered by retractable blinds. *No way a single guy decorated this place.* The window panes rattled from the wind, and Maddie shivered.

Zack pulled her closer. "It's okay, Maddie, you're safe here."

"What if the storm worsens?"

Zack smiled down at her. "The house and windows are built to withstand a category-five hurricane, but if it really gets that bad, there's a storm shelter underneath that we could live in comfortably for a few weeks until it was safe to come out."

"Wow. You're prepared."

"You have no idea." He walked into the attached bathroom. "Let's get you into a shower."

"I think I'd better do that one alone."

Zack set her on her feet and arched an eyebrow. Fire raced through her body. Oh my, he was appealing, but she couldn't let her guard down with a man she didn't know.

"You might fall down again."

"I'll take my chances." She took a step away and threw her shoulders back.

He grinned, his cheeks crinkling irresistibly. "Okay. Make a lot of noise if you fall so I know to come help."

"You are *not* coming to help." Maddie jutted out her chin. "I'll crawl around if I have to."

He chuckled and held up his hands defensively. "Gotcha. I'm going to take my own shower, then." He pointed to the countertop. "There are some clothes, towels, and girly lotion and stuff."

"Thank you." *Thoughtful, wasn't he?*

The door clicked shut. Maddie stripped out of the ruined dress, draping it over the tub to dry, and set the diamond necklace on the counter. She moved slowly as she showered. It felt heavenly to wash her hair with some kind of coconut shampoo. The cut on her forehead only stung when she rinsed it. Thankfully, it wasn't bleeding anymore. After she dried off, she sorted through the pile of clothes and then slipped into a cute romper dress with a colorful red-and-blue pattern. She tightened the waist, but it was still pretty big. There weren't any shoes. Her flimsy heels must've fallen off when she crashed. Maybe she could find them in the morning.

Rubbing some hair serum into her long hair and then brushing it out and moisturizing her face, she almost felt normal again. She eyed herself critically in the mirror. Her skin was tanned enough that it looked fine without makeup, and the eyelash extensions her mom had insisted she get before graduation made her eyes passable, but what she wouldn't give for some lipstick. She rubbed a little hair serum on her lips and found that it made them shine and didn't taste awful. She laughed at herself. It was dumb to be vain when her life was in danger, but Zack was so extremely handsome she wanted to look her best.

When she re-entered the great room, she was impressed to see Zack at the stove wearing a T-shirt and cargo shorts, stirring some boiling noodles and a pot of something that smelled delectable. Her stomach grumbled. She'd been too stressed to realize how hungry she was, and it was late enough that he had to have already eaten. He was very thoughtful. "You cook?"

He turned and smiled. "Can't live by yourself with no McDonald's and not learn." His eyes roved over her. "Sorry, the clothes are big."

"They're wonderful. Thank you."

"Sit down, please, and I'll bring your food." He gestured to a square kitchen table in a nook with even more windows. It seemed the entire house was glass. Rain pattered against the windows, but the wind was calmer now.

"I can help, you know."

"Maybe tomorrow. Tonight, I want you to relax."

Maddie smiled at the thought of still being here tomorrow. She couldn't wait to see the view from these windows. She sat and watched Zack bustle around the large kitchen. Neither of them said anything, but he caught her looking at him and grinned a few times. A lump rose in her throat as she thought back through the night. Gratitude for being safe and regret over her father's wasted life twisted into odd feelings of confusion and a longing to just go home.

Setting a plate of noodles with what looked like homemade marinara and freshly grated parmesan in front of her, Zack dished up his own plate and then sat across from her.

Maddie tried a bite. It was better than the fancy food her father's chef served on the yacht. "You're a good cook. Is this a secret family recipe?"

He chuckled. "Yeah, from the family's hired chef."

"Your mom didn't cook?" She found herself wanting to know more about him.

"No." He laughed again, as if the very thought was humorous. "When she comes to visit, I wait on her hand and foot. She's been so pampered she's not sure how to take care of herself anymore."

"That's oddly sad."

"Isn't it? But she's great. I love having her around." He shook his head and took a drink. "You want to tell me how you ended up in the ocean in a fancy dress all by yourself?"

She studied the bite of noodles, marinara, and Parmesan cheese on her fork. "Um ... no?"

Zack rocked back. He studied her for several long seconds. Maddie fidgeted and thought through every angle. She could lie to him, she could tell him part of the story, or she could trust him. She just wasn't sure where to go with it yet.

"Okay," he finally said.

"Okay?" she echoed, deflating into her chair.

He elevated one shoulder. "You can tell me when you're ready."

Relief poured through her. "Thank you."

"I can take you into Belize tomorrow and help you get where you need to go. Might be a problem with no documents."

"No. I can't go to Belize. I have to go to America." She had no clue why she couldn't go to Belize, but she had to trust that her father wouldn't say that if it wasn't dangerous for her there.

"America!" He shook his head quickly as panic filled his eyes. Maddie hadn't realized how calming his influence was until it was gone, and he was obviously agitated. "I'm sorry, but I'm not taking you to America. I'll help you figure out a way to fly there from Belize or Honduras."

"I can't. My father told me not to go to Belize or Honduras. It's ..." She sighed and finally admitted, "Too dangerous for me."

"Why?"

Maddie paused, then exhaled slowly. "Why don't we sleep on it?"

His eyebrows quirked up.

"I'm not thinking straight. Maybe in the morning I'll be able to explain better."

He nodded but looked unconvinced.

Zack couldn't sleep—hadn't even tried to sleep. This woman had him stirred up in so many different directions he didn't know which way to let his brain go. He was accustomed to his life of productive solitude—

cleaning, cooking, fixing up his house and taking care of the grounds outside, managing his investments via satellite, running, swimming, and reading books. He was happy and didn't need anyone.

Then this beautiful woman crash-landed on his harbor in an evening dress. Part of him wanted to hold her in his arms again, and part of him wanted to throw her off his island. Who would take a fishing boat through an ocean in an evening dress and have no explanation to share? What if she was a lunatic? That might be a best-case scenario, because if she wasn't crazy, she was definitely trouble—the kind of trouble Zack lived alone on an island to avoid. But she'd seemed sane, and she'd felt … nice in his arms. Okay, so much more than nice, but he wasn't going there. It could easily be argued that he was a depraved recluse and any woman would feel more than nice in his arms.

He tiptoed up to her bedroom door for the fifth time. If she found him lurking out here, would she get that panic-stricken look in her eyes again? Leaning close to the door, he simply listened, not sure what he was hoping to hear. Quiet sobbing reached his ears, and he reared back. She was crying. *Dang.* A female creature was bad enough, but a crying one? A weepy kind of woman was scarier to face than America after ruining the entire country's hopes. He turned to leave, but he could almost hear his sister's voice: "Treat women with respect, or I'll kick your can."

He exhaled and couldn't help but smile. He missed Anne more than he would ever admit to anyone. He knocked softly on the door and waited. Finally, a sniffle and a whispered "yes?" came through the door.

"Are you okay? I heard … crying."

She opened the door a crack. The storm had blown over, and all was calm outside, but all was not calm for Maddie. A lamp by the bedside revealed red, puffy eyes. Zack could swear his sister's ghost must've nudged him forward, because no sane man who wanted to stay sane, happy, and alone in the world would walk toward a distraught beauty and enfold her in his arms.

Maddie jerked in surprise as his arms wrapped around her; then she leaned into him, and her arms found their way around him, too. Zack rested his cheek on top of her head and simply held her. After a few minutes, which stirred all kinds of longings and romantic feelings he had no right to be feeling with this stranger, he hoped he'd offered her some kind of comfort. "Do you want to talk about it?"

Maddie bit at her lower lip for a second, then spit out, "I think my father's dead." She shook her head. "I'm pretty sure he's dead."

"I'm sorry." More questions raced through Zack's mind, but he didn't feel it was the right time to ask if that was why she'd shown up on his island. "Were you close to him?"

"Not really. I only saw him a few times growing up. He always took my mom on trips, but never me. He asked me to come to the Caribbean to celebrate graduating with my master's degree. I thought it was going to be this great vacation, but then ..." Her voice trailed off. "Are you close to your father?"

The question was a surprise. Zack's arms fell away from her, and he stepped back. "No. I wish I'd only seen him a few times growing up." He forced a smile and pushed memories of his father back into the closed compartment he thought he'd sealed tight enough that nothing would leak out—especially at moments like this. How would he feel if his father was dead? Probably relieved and guiltier than ever. "Do you think you can sleep now?"

"Probably not, but I really appreciate the, um, comfort."

"Anytime." Zack started. How had he said that and actually meant it? She would be gone in the morning. He'd figure out where he could take her that she deemed safe, and he'd never see her again. There wasn't going to be an "anytime." He backed out of her room, muttered "good night," and fled down the wide hallway.

CHAPTER THREE

Maddie finally crashed early in the morning. She wasn't sure if the insomnia was from worrying about her father and if Bello was coming after her or if it was from the memory of being in Zack's arms. He'd taken care of her without any thought for himself and then comforted her without asking any questions. Just being there. The fact that he was rocking handsome paled in comparison to how kind and understanding he'd been. She'd never felt drawn to a man like this before. There had been plenty of fun boys to date throughout high school and college, and she'd enjoyed flirting, dating, and kissing, but Zack wasn't a boy. He was a man, and she'd already developed a craving to be in his arms again. It was stronger than her craving for her thrice-daily dose of Dr. Pepper. She should check if Zack had any in his fridge.

The sun was already up when she pushed a button on the remote next to her bed, and the privacy blinds retracted. The view was unreal: landscaped gardens and a gorgeous infinity pool and the beach, small harbor, and turquoise ocean beyond. Maybe she should beg Zack to let her stay here rather than try to figure out what was on that flash drive and risk Bello finding her again.

She sighed. She couldn't ask that of Zack, and she would never forgive herself if Bello came and hurt him. Plus, it could become awkward if she tried to overstay her welcome. Bummer. Zack had been very welcoming. He hadn't pushed her to explain or made her feel like she was a burden dropping into his life like this.

Maddie took a quick shower, dressed in a cute thigh-length blue jumper that cinched at her waist, braided her hair out of her face, and walked through the hallway to the great room. The entire house glistened with the sun streaming through the many windows. There were some water spots on the glass from the rain, but besides that, the place was sparkling clean. Did he keep a maid hidden somewhere?

Seeing no sign of Zack in the great room, and really wanting to be outside, she grabbed an apple from a basket of fruit on the counter and walked through the pool area toward the stairs they'd ascended last night. She needed to find Zack and ask if she could borrow some snorkeling gear to look for the package and her shoes.

She finally spotted Zack sprinting on the beach. Stopping mid-bite, she could only stare. Watching him run was poetry in action. *Wow*. He was in a tank top and shorts, and every muscle in his arms, chest, and legs seemed to be engaged. She had never seen a run that beautiful. He looked like an Olympian or something.

Maddie dropped her apple. An Olympian. That's where she'd seen Zack's face before. Zack Tyndale. He was the American athlete who was supposed to win gold in the 110-meter hurdles and 100-meter run in 2012. He'd tripped and fallen in the hurdles finals and been unable to compete in the run. The entire country had moaned in pain with him. *Oh my*. Is that why he was hiding away on this island? Was it too embarrassing to face the American public?

Zack slowed to a walk at the end of the beach by the dock. He glanced up at her, lifted a hand, and smiled a greeting. Maddie made her way down the stairs, clinging to the railing so she didn't trip and fall. Her mom had always called her "my tipsy girl." Falling back into the water last night hadn't been a result of her head injury; it was just another manifestation of her klutziness. She'd gotten used to it and normally didn't embarrass herself.

Zack walked her way with a smile, sweat glistening on his brown skin. *My, oh my, he had a lot of muscles.* She tried not to stare with her mouth open, but craparoni, he was not only fine-looking, but he was famous. How was she supposed to react to that?

"Did you sleep well?" he asked when he reached her.

"You're Zack Tyndale." Her voice was too breathless, like an overexcited fan.

The smile left his face. He nodded slightly. "How did you figure that out?"

"Seeing you run. You're beautiful." She felt heat rushing to her face. "I mean, your run is beautiful."

He inclined his head. His lips turned up, but the smile didn't reach his eyes. "Thank you."

"I watched the Olympics."

"I think the whole world did." He sighed and pushed a hand over his bald scalp.

"Is that why you live in solitude?"

He shrugged. "One of the reasons." He folded his arms over his chest and studied her. "So, you're finding out all of my secrets, how about sharing some of yours? I couldn't sleep making up all kinds of stories. You're a celebrity running from crazed fans. You were on a cruise ship and lost a bet, so you had to deploy a lifeboat. You're a pirate on the wrong side of the battle."

Maddie suddenly found it very hard to breathe or meet his dark gaze. What should she say? He'd been the perfect gentleman. Even when he could've taken advantage of her in her room last night, he'd simply held her and let her cry. Would he want to help her if she spilled her crazy story?

"I came to the Caribbean to spend time with my father." She shook her head. "It was horrible. I realized he's been lying to me all of my life, and the men on his boat were scuzz buckets." She shuddered.

"Scuzz buckets?"

"Yucky dudes who don't brush their teeth and prey on innocents."

Zack's fingers tightened into a fist. "Did they ..." He cleared his throat. "Hurt you?"

"No. My father protected me, but—" She looked over his shoulder and saw something glinting in the ocean. Something large and white.

No. Please, no. Placing a hand to her mouth, she whimpered and glanced back at Zack.

"Hey." Zack touched her arm and shook his head. "I'm sorry. It's okay. We can take this slow. You don't have to tell me until you're ready."

Maddie pointed. "That's my father's yacht." The sleek lines and the Italian flag snapping in the breeze fit the boat from her nightmares last night. She wished she was mistaken, but doubted it very much.

Zack whirled to where she was pointing. He studied the approaching yacht for a second, then said, "And your father's dead?"

She nodded.

"So the people on that yacht?"

"Want me."

"Dead?" His lips flattened and his eyebrows dipped together.

"After they beat and violate me."

"You need to escape."

"Please."

Zack didn't ask any more questions. He grabbed her hand and tugged her toward the stairs. Maddie did her best to keep up. They sprinted through the pool area and into the house. Zack kept her hand in his. Entering a huge master suite, he let go of her hand and ran to the closet. Maddie followed, watching as he opened a safe and pulled out a bundle of money, a passport, and a pistol.

He grabbed her hand again, and they ran down a hallway she hadn't seen before and entered a dark theater room. Zack pushed a lever and a wall moved. Maddie gasped. "What is this?"

Zack actually grinned, grabbing a flashlight from the wall and flicking it on. "I've been waiting for a chance to use this. The previous owner built it in case there was ever trouble. You need to get away before these people find you, right?"

"Yes. But what if they ruin your beautiful home?"

He shrugged. "I can replace it."

Maddie was grateful he didn't seem to be placing blame on her for bringing not only danger but possibly destruction to his peaceful island. She was shocked he would run like this to protect her. If only her father had been half the man Zack was proving himself to be.

"That boat is too big to get into my harbor." He chatted as if they weren't in mortal danger. He directed her through the wall and down a set of stairs. The wall closed behind them. "Stay close," he told her. His hands were full of the things he'd grabbed, so unfortunately, he didn't take her hand. They walked deeper into the earth; the cold made her wish for the sunshine. "They'll have to lower boats to get on the island, and by the time they get here, we'll be long gone. Do you think they tracked you somehow?"

Maddie picked her way down the stairs. She stubbed her pinky toe on the side wall. *Darn having no shoes.* Thankfully, the stairs ended and they entered a level tunnel—less chance of her tripping. "Maybe there was a tracking device on that boat I came on?"

"Maybe," he agreed. "They'll probably see the wreck and know you're here. Do you really think they killed your father?"

"Yes," she whispered. She thought of Bello and shivered. He was coming for her. Just because he wanted the conquest? Or was it because of the flash drive and papers her father had sent with her? The papers! What if they found them by the wreck? Would they think to search it? "Zack!"

He paused and turned to stare at her. The flashlight cast odd shadows off his face.

"They might be after the papers I lost in the water last night."

"Are the papers worth dying for?"

Maddie paused and then shook her head. "I don't care if they get my father's money. At least then they'll leave me alone." She had the information for Homeland Security on the flash drive.

He nodded. "Then let's stick to the plan." He started walking again.

"Which is?"

"This tunnel takes us to my boat. When we speed out of here, I'm betting they follow us, so they might not look for those papers anyway. You don't know what's on them?"

"No, but I have a flash drive in my bra that has the same information."

"O-kay. Seems like a safe place. We definitely don't need the papers if you've got a flash drive."

Maddie grunted her assent, too focused on not tripping in the dark.

The tunnel ended at a door. Zack cautiously opened it and glanced around. "No sign of them. I bet they'll aim their smaller boats for the other dock. While they search the house, we'll escape."

They ran across a large dock and onto his yacht. It was much smaller than her father's, but just as opulent. Zack escorted her into the main cabin. He threw off the mooring lines, then returned and powered up the boat. Within seconds they were cruising out of the harbor. Maddie saw two rubber boats already tied up to the dock and men that had worked for her father jogging up the stairs.

They passed a small boat cruising toward the island. Maddie looked down and met Bello's dark gaze. His eyes narrowed, and anger radiated from him. He pulled a semi-automatic gun out and started shooting. Maddie ducked and screamed. The bullets zinged into the back of the yacht. Zack cursed and upped his speed. More gunshots came, and she could hear Bello screaming for his men to come back. She hoped they would leave Zack's lovely home alone. It made her sick to think of Bello and his men desecrating it, but she didn't want them following her and Zack either.

Within a few minutes, the yacht and Zack's beautiful island were fading behind them. Maddie sank into a captain's chair. "Do you think they'll follow us?"

"If they can catch us." He shook his head. "I should've grabbed my satellite phone."

"What about the radio?"

"It's not secure. We'd have to be really close to America to risk using it." Zack steered the boat with one hand and pinned her with a determined gaze. "It's time you told me the whole story."

CHAPTER FOUR

Z ack studied Maddie sitting in the chair next to his. The early morning sun streamed through the window and highlighted her dark hair with red and gold. He steered the boat to the north, wondering what he was doing. He'd just left his home and island in the clutches of some serious bad guys and raced off in his yacht like a hero to save the beautiful lady. He focused in on her again. Holding her while she cried last night had yanked him into her life whether he wanted to be or not. He had to admit, his life could use a little excitement. A gorgeous woman crash-landing on his island was a good start. Being chased by murderous thugs might be pushing the need for excitement a bit.

Maddie took a deep breath. "I told you I came to the Caribbean to see my father?"

He held up a hand and stopped her before she spilled what must be a very interesting story. "Wait, first we need to set some coordinates. You think the only safe place is the U.S.?"

"That's what my dad said."

"It's less than eight hundred miles to Key West. We can push it at almost forty knots and be there tomorrow." His boat was a Butterfly, one of the fastest yachts in the world. He doubted her father's crew could catch them. The yacht moored next to his island had looked like a Sussurro, which was a lot larger than the Butterfly but not quite as fast. The other boat did have the advantage of more pilots, whereas he'd probably have to stay awake and steer the entire time. He glanced over at Maddie. He'd have to teach her how to pilot the yacht if he wanted a shower or sleep.

"Do you really want to go to America?" she asked. "You seemed ... not happy about it earlier."

Zack shrugged. No, he didn't want to go to America, but it wouldn't kill him to drop her off there. Then he could cruise back to his island and make sure those yahoos didn't destroy anything. Maybe he could take a quick trip to New York and see his niece, but there was no reason to stay stateside long.

He snuck a glance at Maddie again. Some internal instinct told him he'd have a hard time leaving her. She'd still be in danger. Trying to ignore the feeling, he reminded himself that he wasn't some hero; he was an athlete. A washed-up athlete at that.

Typing the coordinates for Key West into the system, he leaned back into the comfortable seat. He was still wearing workout clothes from this morning and could use a shower and some food, but that could wait until after Maddie's story and after he was certain the other boat wasn't pursuing them. Glancing back, he was reassured they were alone. It was a big old ocean; maybe they would get lucky and get out of radar range and never see those guys again.

"Why don't you want to go to America?" Maddie met his gaze, then looked away as if she didn't know if she dared ferret out his secrets.

Zack shook his head. "Uh-uh. Oh no. You're telling me why they're following us first." Even though there was no sign of them, he had an uncomfortable feeling they wouldn't give up easily, especially if they had a 4KW radar system; those could track another boat for fifty miles or more.

Maddie inhaled slowly. "Long version or short?"

Zack laughed. "Long. Did you not hear me just say we're going to be on board for the next twenty-four hours?"

Maddie blinked and her dark eyes brightened. "Thank you. You don't even know me, and you dropped everything to help me. To take me to America."

He had dropped everything, quite literally—his house and his island. But it could all be replaced. Maddie couldn't. "You're welcome. Now talk so I can go shower. I stink."

She wrinkled her nose and smiled. "Your sweat actually smells kind of good to me."

Zack arched an eyebrow, having no clue how to respond to that.

"So, my story." She laced her hands together. "I graduated a couple weeks ago with my master's from Montana State."

"Congratulations."

"Thanks." She gave him a sweet smile, but it disappeared when she continued. "My father invited me to come visit him for a couple of weeks as sort of a graduation present and chance to get to know him."

"You haven't known him?" She didn't say *father* in a very loving voice; obviously there were hurt feelings. He could understand that better than most.

"Not really." She glanced at her hands. "He visited me when it was convenient for him. My mom usually went to meet him somewhere and left me home."

Zack related to the pain in her voice, that feeling of being an accessory that your parent only used when it furthered his ambitions. "Where's your mom?"

"Montana. She raised me alone. I think my dad gave her money, but I don't really know how much support he was, financially or otherwise."

He nodded and stared out at the expanse of ocean—nothing around them for miles. He liked piloting his yacht. Well, except when someone who wanted his passenger dead was following them.

"She always told me my dad was an international businessman, an investor, and had to travel a lot for business." She barked out a laugh. "I can't believe they both lied to me for so long, and I bought it."

"What is your dad, then?" She'd described pretty close to what his father did to amass his own fortune and what Zack had done before he escaped.

"Well, currently, he's probably one of Satan's minions."

Zack smiled, then tried to hide it. She probably wasn't trying to be funny.

Maddie grimaced. "Sorry, that was an inappropriate attempt at humor, but he didn't do much in this life to recommend him to heaven." She wrung her hands together. "You see, he used to be ..." Her voice lowered. "A pirate."

Cold chills ran down Zack's spine. Modern-day pirates were few and far between, but they were vicious and deadly. He'd heard that pirate activity had increased in the Caribbean over the past few months. If the stories were to be believed, the pirates were raping, pillaging, and murdering as viciously as any seventeenth-century crews. Books and movies today tried to make pirates look attractive and funny, but there was nothing cute or praiseworthy about men that caused suffering like this for their own gain. Nothing.

Zack had always felt safe on his island. He obviously needed to be more leery. "How do you know?"

"I heard them talking about yachts they'd attacked. They pretend to be friendly, share their liquor and food, then pull the guns out when it's too late. I guess they're able to take cash, jewelry, make people transfer funds; then they either kill them or leave them to die, depending on if they want their boat or not." She bit at her lip and twisted her hands together.

"But if your father did that for years, surely the authorities would have found him, or we would've heard about it on the news."

"You're right. I think this is a new thing for them, and if I understood them correctly, there's a large group. I think they're associated with the mafia and have been robbing people in different ways for years. Obviously he's always been a crook." She studied her fingernails.

Zack swallowed hard, understanding the heartache this was causing Maddie. His own father had done awful things that he wasn't ready to forgive. "I'm sorry," he offered lamely.

Her head whipped up. "Don't you be sorry. You're taking this huge risk for me." She shook her head. "None of this is your fault, and I really appreciate you taking me in and helping me so much."

"My calendar was open this week."

Maddie laughed. "Lucky me."

Zack grinned and joined in the laughter. "I don't think I'd want your luck right now."

Maddie nodded. "Amen to that."

"So how did you end up on that boat alone?"

She took a long breath. "My father made me go in the boat while he fended off Bello and the other men. I'm just grateful I ended up on your island."

"Me, too."

She gave him a brilliant smile. Wow, she was a beautiful girl. She stood and came right next to him, peering over his shoulder. She smelled nice, clean, and all woman. "Do you want me to drive so you can shower?"

"I knew it. You were lying when you said I didn't stink earlier."

"I never lie. But you said you wanted to shower."

"That would be nice." He stood and gestured her into the seat. "Have you ever steered a boat?"

"Yes. My father taught me this past week."

"Good." He pointed to the display. "Just follow the coordinates northeast, and we'll be set."

"Okay." She nodded, but her eyes were wary. "What if ... they come?"

He didn't need to ask who "they" were. Gesturing out the windows at the expanse of blue, he smiled and lied; no reason to tell her the pirates probably had the best radar money could buy. It was their job to track ships. "It's a big ocean. They don't know where we're going. They're probably drinking my Arizona iced tea on the beach and then filling my swimming pool and house with sand."

Maddie sighed. "I'm so sorry."

"I was just teasing. It'll be fine." He squeezed her arm. The warmth of her flesh seared into him. He was obviously more in need of human interaction than he wanted to admit. Maddie was a beautiful and kind person, but he shouldn't be this affected by a woman he'd just met last night.

"Thank you." Her eyes glistened with unshed tears. "For doing all of this."

Zack nodded and backed away. He spun on his heel and hurried downstairs to the master bedroom. It was either run or take her in his arms. Sweaty and feeling much too attracted to her were not a good combo. She'd probably slap him if he acted on his impulse to ask for a kiss of gratitude—at least if she was smart she would.

CHAPTER FIVE

Maddie maneuvered the boat without paying much attention to anything besides looking behind to make sure the pirates weren't pursuing them. Every so often she check that they were heading in the right direction. It was really too easy—if she hadn't been so afraid of what might be coming. She needed something to distract her from thinking about her father's death and the evil men now chasing her.

She thought of Zack. Okay, maybe not that big of a distraction. Oh, man, he was one fine-looking dude. It was amazing that he would drop everything and put himself in danger for her. He probably would've been in more danger if he'd stayed on the island to greet Bello, but Zack hadn't known that. What if he'd just assumed Bello was another rich guy coming to visit? Zack was amazing. He'd believed her and jumped into action. She couldn't think when a man had trusted her word and protected her without a thought. Her father definitely had never done either. Her last boyfriend, Robert, had expected a trophy if he opened the door as they walked into a building.

She thought of Bello, and chills raced down her arms. She glanced back for the twentieth time and, thankfully, saw nothing in the ocean behind them. Blowing out a long breath, she said a quick prayer of gratitude that they were safe and continued begging for protection. If only they could get to America. Touching the flash drive in her bra, she wished it was time to turn it over to the authorities and be done with this nightmare. Would Bello keep chasing her once they got to America?

She smelled fresh man before she heard him. Whirling, she smiled at Zack. He'd shaved, and her fingers itched to touch the masculine lines of his jaw. *Yummy.* "You move too quiet."

"Runner." He shrugged. "Have to be light on my feet. I'm going to find some food. Are you hungry?"

Maddie was too nervous to think about food. "Not really, too scared." She shouldn't have admitted that. "But I should probably eat something."

Zack squeezed her arm. Her stomach smoldered from the warmth of his touch. "I'll see what I can find."

She appreciated that he didn't give empty assurances that she shouldn't be nervous. Pirates were probably chasing them, and she knew better than he did how awful they were. Bello's leering smile was imprinted in her memory. She swallowed hard and tried to focus on steering the boat straight.

It was an absolutely beautiful yacht. The interior was all light wood and windows with chrome and dark wood accents. The captain's chairs and furniture were white leather, plush and comfy. The back opened up onto a magnificent deck with more seating and an outdoor table. Maddie wished they weren't running for their lives so she could just enjoy the opulence and relaxation such a boat offered. She really wished she could go back to Zack's island and explore and enjoy that beautiful setting and home for a week, or maybe a month.

This yacht and the island both told a story about this intriguing and handsome man. He was obviously wealthy and enjoyed beautiful things. There was a peaceful and warm feeling on this boat, just like there had been in his house. Such a contrast from the equally opulent yacht she'd been on the past week and a half. Both were absolutely beautiful, but Zack's felt welcoming and homey. She prayed Bello and his men hadn't damaged Zack's spot of paradise and wouldn't find them on his boat. If they could make it to America, hopefully she and

Zack would be safe. Even though she didn't know him well, she didn't like the idea of leaving him once they reached safety.

Zack returned with a box of crackers, granola bars, and water bottles. "Sorry. I usually stock the boat better when I go on a trip. I'm not very prepared to take care of a lady."

"You're sorry?" Her voice pitched up. The nerves and worry all compounded with her gratitude to him. She would be raped and dead if he hadn't intervened. He had absolutely no right to apologize for being so good to her. "You've just deserted your beautiful house to pirates and risked your life to help me, and *you're* sorry." Maddie flung herself into his arms and kissed him. His lips were full and warm. She pulled back just as quickly. "Man, oh, Pete. Now *I'm* sorry."

"*You're* sorry?" Zack repeated with a big grin splitting his handsome face. "You just made my month, and *you're* sorry?" He pulled her back into his arms and kissed her, long and slow and passionately.

Maddie was breathing hard when he released her lips. "Nobody's driving the boat," she whispered.

Zack laughed. "I've got more important things to do than steer a boat."

She arched an eyebrow at him as he lowered his head and took possession of her mouth once again.

They broke apart with equally large grins and shortness of breath. Zack offered her a granola bar. He took the captain's chair while they both ate their simple breakfast. Maddie worried she'd made it more than awkward with her impulsive kiss, but Zack was smiling and relaxed and acted like women spontaneously kissed him in gratitude every day. She glanced at his handsome profile. They probably did ... when he was around women.

"Why do you live all alone?" she asked.

Zack's smile slipped. He took a slow drink from his water bottle, then set it in the cup holder. "Don't like people."

Maddie cocked her head to the side and studied him. "Liar. If that was true, you would've kicked me off your island instead of helping me."

Zack grinned and splayed his hands. "I said I don't like people. I like gorgeous brunettes."

Maddie flushed and took a sip of water. "Would you tell me the truth?"

"About thinking you're beautiful? I just did."

"Thank you." She savored the compliment for a second. He was a breathtaking man, and he was complimenting her. She finally got brave enough to ask. "Will you tell me the truth about why an Olympic athlete is living on a tropical island hundreds of miles from civilization? Did you leave because of the 2012 Olympics?" Maddie was being too pushy, but she felt like he needed to share as much as she wanted to know.

Zack's throat bobbed as he swallowed. He studied the ocean in front of them. "That was part of it. I never liked all the recognition and fame." He glanced at her. "Please don't bring up the *Rising Star* thing. My dad conned me into doing the photo shoot."

Maddie's eyes widened. She'd forgotten. "That was you?" Of course it was. She brought a hand to her lips and couldn't help the small giggle that escaped. Had she really just kissed the Most Beautiful Man in America for 2012? He'd been on the front cover of the *Rising Star* magazine. All those pictures of him shirtless or in tailored suits. How could she have forgotten? She and every female student at MSU had drooled over that article. Her friends would die of jealousy, especially her closest friend, Abby, who had been obsessed with Zack for a while. "Wait. You had hair then."

"Yes." He rubbed at his head, and his lower lip protruded a little bit. "You're seriously laughing at my misfortune?"

"Misfortune to be the Most Beautiful Man in America? Oh, wow, somebody is overconfident. That must've been really hard on you."

"You have no idea." His hand resting on the steering wheel became a vice grip as he stared out the window.

"Honestly." She stopped laughing at him. "It was hard on you?"

He gave her a partial smile. "Before that, I was just a wealthy athlete, and the attention was manageable. After that, it was disgusting. Women throwing themselves at me. My niece being exposed to slimy women who wanted to get to me through her. Even her preschool teachers tried to take advantage of her."

That did sound awful. She felt like a snake for laughing at him. "You have a niece?"

"Yeah, she's my favorite person in the world."

But his face looked so sad when he said it. Probably because his sister was gone. Maddie's heart broke for him. "How old is she?"

"Four."

"That's a fun age."

He nodded. "Wish I could see her more." He cleared his throat and shook out the hand that had been gripping the steering wheel.

Maddie wanted to ask more about his niece. It was obviously his choice he didn't live by her and see her more, but maybe that wasn't the smartest thing to point out to her handsome rescuer. She decided to redirect. "So all these women start throwing themselves at you, then the, um, thing happened at the Olympics."

"Me tripping and losing my status as America's hope?"

"Yeah, that." Oh, how she empathized with him. She'd worked really hard to cure her klutziness—dance classes, learning how to slalom ski, standing on one foot for what seemed like hours—but she still tripped occasionally. Okay, more than occasionally. "So did that cure the women coming after you?"

"Oh, no. They just changed their ploys to act like it was out of sympathy."

Maddie knew the chagrined look on his face wasn't fake. He really did hate the attention. "Most men would be thrilled to have women throwing themselves at them."

He shook his head. "They should try it for a while. It's never the type of women you want throwing themselves at you. The nice, natural beauties, like you, aren't lining up to proposition someone because he's famous."

Maddie's cheeks warmed. He thought she was nice and a natural beauty? Should she thank him?

He continued before she could say anything. "Sorry. I'm probably sounding so cocky, and I'm really not. Well, I hope I'm not."

"No, I shouldn't have said you're overconfident. I didn't realize what something like that would do to somebody's life. I'm sorry."

"Thanks."

"So living in exclusion was all about getting away from women, and then I showed up. Did you think I was some crazed fan coming to find you?" She'd thrown herself at him every which way. Landing on his island. Hugging him in the dark last night. Kissing him a few minutes ago. Her face burned with embarrassment.

Zack laughed. "I never thought of that. Are you?"

"I wish. Sadly, my story is true."

Zack arched an eyebrow. "Yeah. I've seen the proof of that."

They both fell silent at the remembrance of what they left on the island. Maddie needed to break the heaviness of the moment. "But I'm happy to be with the Most Beautiful Man in America now."

"Even better that you got to kiss him. You can tell all your friends."

The moment went slow and sticky as their eyes locked, and Maddie wanted to kiss him again. Bragging to her friends wasn't even in the top five reasons of why she wanted to kiss him. "For a tipsy girl, I'm a lucky schmuck."

Zack grunted out a surprised laugh. "You're a tipsy girl? Do you drink a lot?"

"Don't need to drink. Natural clumsiness. That's why I fell off the dock last night." She really needed to curb her tongue. Here he was the Most Beautiful Man in America, and she was a clumsy little girl who threw herself at him.

"I'm betting the bump on your head and the stress of the night didn't help."

She appreciated his understanding. "I guess that could've been a factor."

"Is your head better?"

"Yes. Thanks. It hardly bled." She touched it. "Just a little tender." She couldn't hold his warm gaze much longer without throwing herself into his arms again. She didn't blame all those women who threw themselves at him, not one bit. Though, she did hate the idea of anyone but her kissing those full, yummy lips.

Gathering up their wrappers and the boxes of granola bars and crackers, she walked back to the kitchen area, threw the garbage away, and set the boxes on the counter. She walked slowly through the beautiful main area and out onto the back patio. The ocean stretched out behind them and was thankfully empty of any other boats.

Settling onto a plush couch, she leaned back and soaked in the sun on her face. The wind softly blew around her, and she closed her eyes. A few minutes without staring at Zack would be the only way she could keep herself in check right now.

CHAPTER SIX

Zack watched Maddie go until she settled onto one of the outdoor couches. He liked talking with her, but didn't mind the break. If she hadn't made the quip about her landing on his island and being a tipsy girl, he might've revealed the main reason he'd run from America. He didn't know her very well, yet he was telling all his secrets and kissing her. He smiled. That kiss had been more than worth any discomfort it may have caused. Maybe before they parted ways, he'd get another kiss of gratitude.

He couldn't believe he'd brought up the article, being touted as the Most Beautiful Man in America, and all the women acting so nuts around him. What an idiot. She probably did think he was a cocky jerk.

He was grateful to be away from starry-eyed, fake women making passes at him, but the real reason he'd escaped America was so he wouldn't be forced into working with his dad. Sadly, he actually liked the work. He liked being in the business world clashing brains with some of the smartest people he knew, and working out solutions. Yet he hated being his father's puppet. After he failed at the Olympics, and it was demanded of him that he take his rightful place with Tyndale Enterprises, he'd run.

He'd started working for his father at age fourteen and had been extremely smart with the money he'd earned. His father had paid him on commission to make him work harder. Big mistake on his father's part. Zack took the large sums of money he earned and learned everything he could about investing. By the time he graduated from NYU, he'd amassed a very nice nest egg, and had quit working for his father. Throughout the years of training for the Olympics, he'd mostly let his money grow. He'd taken a big chunk when he left the States and bought his island and the yacht. He could live comfortably for the rest of his life without working another day. Yet, he had to admit that he missed the business world and the energy and challenge of interacting with other people.

After making sure the boat was on course, he grabbed a fresh bottle of water out of the fridge and went to check on Maddie. She was sleeping peacefully, stretched out on the couch in the sunlight. Man, she was beautiful. Without a stitch of makeup and wearing his sister's too-big dress, she was one of the most breathtaking women he'd ever seen. The dress showed off her shapely shoulders and legs.

Forcing himself to stop staring, he turned to go back inside. A glint of white caught his eye. He squinted, then ran for the binoculars. Returning within seconds, he pressed the binoculars to his eyes and cursed. It was a white yacht, big enough to be the men who chased them. They must have top-of-the-line radar. Zack's heart rate bumped up.

"Maddie." He shook her shoulder.

"Yeah?" She stretched and sat up. "Sorry. I didn't mean to ditch you and then fall asleep. This couch is just so comfy."

"It's okay." He rushed the words out and handed her the binoculars. "Is that your father's boat?"

Maddie's eyes widened. She jumped to her feet and stared through the lenses. "Yes," she whispered.

Zack sprinted back to the captain's seat and jammed the throttle forward. They were going just under forty knots, but he could kick it up to almost fifty. The other yacht shouldn't be as fast because it was so much bigger. His was built for speed, but he couldn't maintain this pace all the way to Key West. And, with their radar equipment, they could follow him and Maddie anywhere. He glanced at the beautiful woman who seemed to trust that he would protect her. What were they going to do? He couldn't physically run from the pirates, and he didn't think his business negotiation skills were going to be effective.

Maddie was by his side, staring back through the open doors. "Will they catch us?"

"They shouldn't be able to." He squeezed her hand, hoping he looked confident. "My boat is definitely faster, but we can't maintain this speed long enough to get to America. We'll have to try to hide."

"Where?"

"I have a friend in Cozumel." He almost smiled thinking of his hilarious friend, Brooks. Then his smile disappeared as he realized Brooks would be hitting on Maddie nonstop, and if she was anything like any other female Zack knew, she'd fall for Brooks within minutes of meeting him. The women always came for Zack initially, but Brooks' charm swayed them pretty quickly.

"Okay," she whispered.

Zack pulled her against his side. "It's okay, Maddie. I'll protect you."

She clung to him. Zack felt all his protective male instincts fire. His rational mind was telling him to slow down, but the beast inside was telling him he'd fight with everything he had to keep her safe. Maddie glanced up at him, and he wished they weren't being chased by pirates so he could kiss the daylights out of her.

She gave him a squeeze, then released him. Zack felt the loss, but knew he needed to focus. He reconfigured the coordinates for the small island of Cozumel, just east of Cancun, instead of blowing past it.

"How long?" she asked quietly.

"About two hours."

She blew out a breath. "Guess I'd better get praying."

"Don't worry." He flashed her a confident smile that he didn't really feel. "This boat is so fast, they won't even know where we've gone."

Seeing her father's boat behind them brought back all the terror of last night, and Maddie had to swallow to keep the granola bar down. Her breaths came in little pants. She couldn't face forward but stared continuously out the back, praying and hoping that the boat wouldn't gain on them.

What would Bello do to Zack? She gnawed at her lip. She'd gotten Zack into this, even though she hadn't meant to, and now he was in danger. She glanced at the chiseled features of his face. He was more handsome than any man she'd been around, but there was so much depth to him. He'd helped her without thinking of his own safety or the cost to his property. To return the favor, she brought more misery down on him.

Zack caught her eye and motioned her to his side. He gently ran one hand down her arm. "It's okay, Maddie. We'll lose them. I promise."

"How can you be so sure?" She hated that her voice was so shaky. Zack had to know how terrified she was, and that wasn't going to help him or the situation.

"Because I made sure to have one of the fastest boats around."

Maddie forced a smile. She wanted to beg him to hold her again, but she stayed strong and walked toward the open back area. Squinting out into the ocean, she couldn't see the boat anymore. A wave of relief swept over her, but she couldn't quite relax. Picking up the binoculars that Zack had left sitting on the table, she searched and searched and finally saw a white shape behind them.

Zack was right about the speed of his boat. For the next hour, she paced and stared through the binoculars, but she couldn't see any sign of the other boat. Maddie felt her racing heart calm. Maybe they really could ditch Bello at Cozumel and then keep going to America. Maybe he wouldn't kill them both. The thought of him hurting Zack brought a sting of tears to her eyes. It would be all her fault.

She rejoined Zack in the cabin. Though she couldn't relax, she was able to sit and sip from a bottle of water and talk to Zack about his Olympic training. And she shared her experiences playing high school and college volleyball and the hard work and enjoyment she'd found in that. Volleyball had started as another quest not to be clumsy, but she'd grown to love it and been good enough to walk onto the college team and play a fair amount.

Zack pointed out the window and she about cried with relief to see land coming up on their left—or portside, as her father would have corrected. Surprised again at the sorrow she felt for her father, Maddie hoped that something on the flash drive would give her some explanation of why he acted the way he did.

They followed the Mexican coastline for a while before they saw the island of Cozumel. Zack maneuvered his boat expertly into a yacht club. "I come here often enough that the port authorities won't do a thorough check of my boat. You'll need to go down below while they board and talk to me, though. People who work in ports have this crazy obsession with passports."

Panic tightened Maddie's chest. "What if they check the whole boat or see me when we get off?" She hadn't thought about dealing with Mexican authorities, only being safe from Bello.

"They know I'm a loner." His cheek crinkled. "Plus, Mexican government isn't as regulated as America. For a little cash they'll always look the other way."

"Here's praying."

"You do that." Zack smiled encouragingly at her.

Maddie hurried down the steps and went to the farthest bedroom. Just to be safe, she slid into the closet and closed it. Maybe she was being melodramatic, but if they searched the boat and found her, she didn't think it would bode well for her or Zack.

Footsteps sounded above her head. She strained, but couldn't understand their conversation. Did Zack know Spanish? Maddie was grateful for Zack's quiet confidence, because she was a nervous wreck as she wrung her hands together and waited in the dark. Even though it was cool down here, sweat beaded on her forehead and chest. She bowed her head and muttered a prayer for help over and over again. The boat engine started, and she could feel the soft vibrations as it moved. What did that mean? Did the port authorities reject them? She didn't dare leave her safe spot.

A few minutes later, the boat stopped and the motor cut. The lack of circulation and the heat that had built in the small space had perspiration dripping down her back. She held perfectly still and imagined worst-case scenarios, trying to believe that Zack would do the right thing for her. He had so far, but experience with her father and other men had taught her that trust was a dumb thing to give them. What if she'd pushed too far kissing Zack like she had when he had flat-out admitted his disgust of women who threw themselves at him? What if he'd stopped at Cozumel so he could turn her over to the authorities and jet back to his island?

Footsteps came again, and Maddie's entire body tensed when the door to the room she was hiding in opened. They were coming for her. She scrunched into the back of the closet, wishing there were clothes or something to hide behind. Closing her eyes, she panted for breath and prayed more fervently.

"Maddie?" Zack called.

All her breath rushed out. He was here. She pushed open the closet door.

"Hey." His face was filled with concern. "You okay?"

"Yes, I just ... got scared." She tripped as she came out of the closet, but Zack was there to steady her. His strong arms held her up, and she wanted to lean into him and not let go. The past week and a half she'd had no peaceful familiarity, no one to talk to or comfort her. In less than twenty-four hours she'd become as comfortable with Zack as she was with any of her friends from home, and once again he'd proven he was there for her.

Zack pulled her closer and simply held her. "Everything's good," he said against her forehead. "The authorities cleared me, and I requested an out-of-the-way spot so we can get off the boat without drawing attention. If the guys following you somehow come to the island, they'll have a hard time finding the boat."

"Thank you," she whispered. Maddie lifted her head and glanced at his handsome face. "You're a smartie and a very upstanding guy, you know that?"

Zack chuckled. "I haven't heard that often, but thank you."

Maddie straightened. "You should hear it more. You're amazing. Sacrificing so much for someone you don't even know."

His eyebrows arched in a teasing way. "I know a little about you. You're fun to talk to and even more fun to kiss."

Maddie laughed, but the lightness faded away as his gaze held hers, and she felt warm and light-headed from the depth in his eyes. Was it possible he was as interested in her as she was in him? Could this be real, or was it just the result of being thrown together in a high-intensity situation and having no choice but to rely on each other? Maybe these feelings were just superficial and would fade as soon as they parted.

His head lowered toward hers, and Maddie wanted to slow down time and savor the way he seemed to desire her. Their lips connected. His full mouth maneuvered hers in a pattern that was both as heady as riding a rollercoaster and inhaling the scent of lilacs in the springtime. Maddie clung to him. Zack released her lips and his hold on her. He took her hand. "We'd better get going."

She nodded, unable to think or speak after that kiss. They made their way through the boat and out into the bright sunshine. Maddie was impressed with his foresight, as they were between several larger yachts on an out-of-the-way ramp. Trees butted right up to the water, their thick foliage making her feel even more hidden. Bello would have to search every slip to find their boat.

She kept her head down and hurried along beside Zack, hoping no one would stop them and question where another passenger came from on his boat.

Zack squeezed her hand. "It's going to be great. We just have to get into town and rent something to go to Brooks' house."

"How far is town?"

"About two miles south of here."

"Two miles?" She didn't mind walking or running, but without shoes it would be miserable. She also wanted to be safely at his friend's house as soon as possible in case Bello showed up.

"We'll find a ride. We're lucky like that."

Maddie nodded, focusing on positive thoughts. "We have been lucky, haven't we?"

"I know I have been. You landed on my island." He smiled at her.

"Thank you." He was so great. How blessed had she been to find someone like Zack last night? Maybe her father wasn't in Hades and was guiding her as a guardian angel or something.

They walked through the busy yacht club, and Zack found a taxi driver to take them into town. As they settled into the musty-smelling car, she whispered, "Why don't we just have him take us to your friend's?" She was dying to be somewhere safe. A heavy fear pressed down around her like being forty feet underwater without scuba gear. *Zack will protect me, Zack will protect me*, she kept repeating to herself.

"I like to have my own car. Plus I don't want anyone seeing where we go, just in case."

She understood his logic, but it still seemed like too long to be exposed.

They drove along a two-lane road with the ocean on one side and thick foliage on the other. Occasionally, Maddie would glimpse an opening in the trees and a building or hotel. Within minutes they were in the middle of what she assumed was the main street of town. The ocean was still to her left, but the other side now housed shops stacked on top of and next to each other. Everything from jewelry to hammocks was displayed. Traffic slowed to a crawl. "Cruise ship," the driver muttered, gesturing out his window.

There were several massive cruise ships docked in the port, and the people spilling down their ramps clogged up the streets with rental cars, taxis, bikes, and pedestrians.

"It's okay," Zack said. "We can walk through the market to the rental shop." He pressed some money into the driver's hands, and he pulled over to the curb. They both slipped out Zack's side of the car.

Maddie scanned the busy street, seeing all kinds of bright clothing, sunglasses, and toys for sale. Shopkeepers shouted lower and lower prices when an American walked away from a deal. She wished they were tourists and could enjoy the sunny day and bartering for treasures, but it definitely wasn't that moment. Glancing back at the cruise ships, she saw a yacht making its way into the harbor and up to a massive stone pier. A white yacht with an Italian flag. She gripped Zack's arm, the terror washing over her anew. How could her father's yacht have followed them here? It didn't seem possible, but that was definitely Bello and his men.

"What?" He glanced at her. "You okay?"

She pointed.

Zack's eyes widened, and he cursed under his breath. "They followed us here instead of into the yacht club," Zack muttered as the yacht sailed right into the harbor. "Their radar should've taken them to the yacht club. That's why I came here."

Radar? How would Zack know if they had radar?

They backed away and hid behind a street vendor's cart, the smell of cinnamon and grease unsettling Maddie's stomach. Zack peeked around the cart at the boat.

"The flash drive." Zack whirled on her. "It has to be the flash drive. Unless they've bugged you." His eyes swept over her. He lifted her hair and probed her neck.

"Nobody's bugged me. What are you *doing*?"

"Looking for some kind of incision. Did they knock you out or drug you at any time you were on that ship?"

"No. I think I would remember that." Maddie felt like she was in some sci-fi movie. Could somebody have injected a bug into her without her knowing it?

Zack's lips thinned. "Give me the flash drive, Maddie. We've got to get rid of it."

"I can't." She placed her hand over her breast as if to protect all she had left of her father. "It's got the information I need to give to the authorities. I'll never be safe from Bello without it."

Zack exhaled slowly and glanced back out at the ocean. The pirates were getting closer. Their boat aligned with the dock. An authority ran up to their boat, gesturing with his arms. "They shouldn't be able to dock there," Zack said.

They both watched as some money exchanged hands, and the authority walked away.

"What about that packet?" Zack whirled back to face her. "You said it had the information, too."

"It's under the water back at your island!"

"We'll double back and use my snorkeling or scuba gear to find it. We have to get rid of that flash drive. Now. We can still make it to Brooks' house. When it's safe, we'll take his boat or mine back to the island and find that packet. Then I'll take you wherever you want to go. If they're not tracking us, we can lose them easily."

Maddie closed her eyes and prayed. She had to trust Zack. He'd proved himself trustworthy, and honestly, he was all she had.

She pulled the flash drive out and placed it in his hand. He squeezed her hand briefly. "Stay here." Running for the pier, he ducked low to avoid Bello's group seeing him, even though they shouldn't be able to recognize him from the brief glimpse they'd gotten as they passed boats this morning. Zack got in the middle of a group of tourists. Maddie saw him slip the flash drive into an older lady's oversized beach bag. He hurried back to Maddie and grabbed her hand. "Let's go."

"What about that poor lady?"

He frowned. His brow furrowed. "They'll recognize as soon as they see her that she's not you."

"I hope they don't hurt her."

"Me too." His grip tightened.

They speed-walked away from the harbor and toward a street filled with small shops packed with merchandise. Little pebbles irritated the soles of Maddie's feet, but she tried not to let that show. Zack had been so good to her; he didn't need to listen to her complain.

Maddie heard some shouts behind them and about fainted when she recognized Bello's men. Oh no. Zack's plan didn't work. They weren't following the lady. Could Maddie possibly have a bug in her body or something crazy like that? Wouldn't she have known? She'd locked her door every night and was a light sleeper. Could they have drugged her and she didn't even remember?

"They're coming," she told Zack.

He glanced back and upped their speed. They ducked into a shop that featured hundreds of beautiful sundresses. Zack tugged her toward the back of the shop and a dressing room. He pulled a few hundred-dollar bills out and gave them to the young female shopkeeper. "Can you bring her a few pretty dresses to try on and some comfortable sandals?" He looked to Maddie. "Size ..."

"Four for the dress. Seven shoes."

The shopkeeper nodded.

"And if anyone comes looking in here, you didn't see us." He added a couple more hundreds.

She smiled. "Got it."

Zack grinned at her and pulled the curtain closed behind them. Maddie's heart was thumping out of control. "How are we going to get away?" She panted for air.

Zack enfolded her in his strong arms. "Let's get you changed into something different and maybe a hat to hide that pretty hair." He tilted his head to the side and smiled at her.

Maddie took long, slow breaths, thankful for Zack's calm presence. How was he not freaking out when those men were still tracking them? "Maybe we should get a hat to hide your lack of hair and that handsome, famous face."

He chuckled at that. "Good idea."

The girl brought several long, flowing dresses and some strappy white sandals. Zack released Maddie and turned his back so she could change.

Suddenly, they heard loud voices out in the store. Maddie slipped a dress over her head just as Zack turned to her. He pulled her into his arms, and they waited in tense silence. After several charged seconds, Maddie wasn't sure if she could take the stress much longer. Wasn't there a back door or somewhere they could run? This standing and waiting was killing her.

The voices faded, then disappeared. Maddie left the clothes she'd been wearing in the dressing room and slid on the sandals. The red-and-white-striped sundress molded to her curves, and she felt prettier than she had since taking a plunge into the ocean last night.

Zack glanced up and down her body. "That looks great on you."

"Thanks."

They crept around the curtain, and the girl smiled at them. "I told them I no see you."

"Thank you." Zack returned the smile. "Do you have something that can hide her hair and a hat for me?"

"Yes." She found a cool turban thing to twist Maddie's hair up into and a wide-brimmed straw hat for Zack. He exchanged his T-shirt for a floral print shirt, and they were as disguised as they could be. He pulled out his wallet, but the girl waved him off. "You give me plenty." She strode out onto the street and looked around for a while before returning. "Men are gone. Vayanse."

"Thanks." Zack took Maddie's hand and led her out of the shop. The warm sun wasn't the only reason sweat trickled down her back as they walked through the busy market. Maddie would've loved to stop and look in the little shops, but the terror of Bello finding her drove her on. Her eyes darted around, looking for anyone familiar.

"How far do we need to go?" she asked.

"On the other side of the market there's a place we can rent a Jeep; then we'll be at Brooks' house in twenty minutes tops."

"You're sure his house will be safe?"

Zack glanced down at her with a reassuring smile and squeezed her hand. "Very safe. He takes his protection pretty seriously."

Maddie could almost taste safety. Twenty minutes and they'd be with Zack's friend. She searched in front of them and then chanced a glance behind. A man with long, dark hair and a goatee strode toward them. It was Jericho.

"Zack. One of them is coming up behind us."

Zack didn't even look behind them. He pulled her into an alleyway between stores, took his hat off and pulled it down to cover both of their faces. Then he kissed her. Maddie's body melted into his, and if she wasn't so terrified, she would've savored his amazing kiss. They were intertwined, giving and taking comfort and desire, when Maddie felt a breeze. She could feel Jericho's breath on her neck and knew he was trying to get a glimpse of them under the hat. Maybe he'd think she was just a local because of her dark skin. She pressed harder into Zack so Jericho wouldn't get a clear view of her face.

"Leave those two alone," another voice came. "Would you want someone interrupting your makeout?" He laughed. Maddie thought it might be Jack, one of the more ruthless pirates who had terrified her even before she'd realized what they all were. "Bello just called, and the girl is on the ferry going to the mainland."

Maddie clung to Zack, kissing him as if she didn't even know the men were there. Jericho dropped Zack's hat and backed away.

Maddie sagged against Zack in relief. It *had* been the flash drive that was bugged, not her. Zack grinned at her, and gave her one more soft kiss. "If I'd known being scared would produce a kiss like that, I would've gone running for the pirates."

Maddie smacked his solid chest. "Not funny."

Zack put the hat back on his head and took her hand again. "I wasn't joking."

Maddie shook her head but didn't answer. Zack led her through the crowds to a small shop with scooters and Jeeps out front. The man greeted Zack with a back-thumping hug and a rush of Spanish. Zack replied; apparently he did know the language. The man gestured to Maddie and grinned. "Ella es muy hermosa," he said.

Zack nodded to her. "Yes, she is very, very beautiful."

Maddie gave a self-deprecating laugh, but her chest warmed at his compliment. What would he think if he saw her with her hair done and makeup on? She hoped she'd have the chance to really fix herself up for him someday.

Zack continued conversing in Spanish, signed some papers, and handed over a couple hundred-dollar bills. He seemed to have an endless supply of those. They hadn't gotten into what he'd done to be at a financial level where money didn't seem to be an issue to him. He'd said something about being a wealthy athlete earlier. Maddie wished she could sit and talk to him with no agenda or worry of Bello's men finding them. She needed to keep showing him gratitude for all he was doing for her. She flushed at the thought.

Within minutes they were loaded into a red Jeep. Zack drove down some rutted side streets and popped out onto the main street a few blocks from the busy section of town. Maddie glanced back, but couldn't see her father's yacht. Had they left? They thought Maddie was on the ferry, so maybe they were chasing it. That would give Maddie and Zack more time to escape if Bello had to get to the mainland before he found the flash drive.

She relaxed against the seat. "You were right. It was the flash drive."

Zack gripped the steering wheel. "Didn't your father give that to you?"

Had her father set her up? But why try to help her escape in the first place? "Yes. Bello must've known about it. Maybe he set up the tracking device on it somehow or found something in my father's things. Maybe he tortured the information out of my father." She swallowed.

"Maybe." Zack didn't say anything more. He pulled off his hat and tossed it onto the backseat.

She felt a flush of shame that her father had associated with such horrible men. She wished she could ask him why he'd involved her in this mess. Maybe when they found those papers she would have her answers. She wasn't sure if she wanted them or not.

Pulling the wrap off of her hair, she finger-combed the long curls and stared out the side of the Jeep. The foliage was thick. The green reminded her of home, except the trees here were mostly palms instead of pine trees. Glimpses of the ocean and beach beyond were nothing like home, though. Vacationers riding scooters honked at them and waved gleefully as they passed. Maddie smiled and waved back, but such lightheartedness seemed a lifetime away for her. Had it really only been two weeks ago she'd been celebrating with her friends and Mom when she graduated?

Zack turned down a paved road. A huge gate appeared before them, and a guard holding a gun that meant business strolled out to meet them. She guessed it was a machine gun, but really had no clue. Her only exposure to guns was the occasional shoot-'em-up flick that a date would take her to and her dad teaching her how to use a handgun when she was a teenager. Zack greeted the man in Spanish like they were old friends. The man smiled, but didn't release his grip on the weapon or seem overly friendly.

The gate swung open, and they drove a couple hundred yards down the asphalt driveway. The trees fanned out to reveal a stucco mansion and the beach beyond. Zack had barely shoved the Jeep into neutral and pulled up the parking brake when a man bounded out of the house. He didn't look quite as tall as Zack, but he was thicker, with ropy muscles like a bodybuilder. His dark hair was longer, and his face was tan, but he was obviously not a native Mexican.

"My boy!" he hollered.

Maddie laughed. "You're his boy?"

Zack shook his head. "Get ready. You're about to be mauled."

"What?" Her eyes darted around looking for a large dog or something. Mauled by what?

Zack jumped out of the Jeep and hugged his friend. Maddie slid out of her side and walked around to meet this over exuberant guy. He pulled back from the hug with Zack and glanced over at Maddie. His jaw slackened for a second before he thumped Zack on the back. "Whoa. You scored for yourself, son."

Maddie was certain this guy wasn't that much older than Zack, but he kept calling him *boy* and *son*. So weird. She stuck out her hand. "Hi, I'm Madeline."

He brushed past the hand and pulled her into a hug. She caught a whiff of expensive cologne as her face pressed into his bulging pecs. Too much money and too much time hitting the gym were obvious obsessions with this guy. He pulled back and grinned, revealing ultra-white teeth and a smile that most women probably melted over and gave her a quick kiss on the mouth.

"Whoa!" Maddie backed away.

Zack was shaking his head. He came to her rescue, pulling her into his side. "She's my girl, Brooks."

Maddie stared up at Zack. She was tempted to refute that and explain that they'd barely met, but she wondered if she needed the protection from his friend. Zack thought she would be safe here?

"Nice! Good for you." Brooks clapped his large hands together, jerking his thumbs toward his chest. "Brooks Johnson. It's nice to meet you, Madeline."

"Maddie," she murmured, wrapping her arm around Zack's back, liking the feel of him close to her.

"Maddie," Brooks repeated. "Well, come in, come in. You hungry? Ready to swim? Snorkel? Get a massage? We could take the speedboat out and parasail. Great way to see my island."

Maddie's head was whirling.

"I'm starving," Zack said.

"Perfect. Dinner is almost ready."

A butler of sorts greeted them at the door, a dark-skinned young man wearing loose-flowing cotton slacks and a button-down shirt. He shook Zack's hand and smiled at Maddie.

"Can you stay for a while?" Brooks asked as he gestured them into the two-story foyer.

"Um, we're not sure?" Zack glanced at her. Maddie lifted a shoulder. She didn't know if they should be running or staying put. If Zack thought they were safe here, maybe they should stay, but her instinct was to get away from this island and any chance of running into Bello or his men.

"You can't turn down my hospitality." Brooks looked like they'd just scalped his cat.

"Maddie needs ... my help." Zack arched an eyebrow at her as if asking permission to share her story. Maddie shook her head slightly. She didn't know this guy. It was scary enough to trust Zack, who had proven himself trustworthy and brave since she'd landed on his island. Brooks might be Zack's friend, but he seemed really loud and a little unstable. Zack turned his attention back to Brooks. "Can you give us a minute?"

"Sure." Brooks' voice was laden with pain, as if Maddie's lack of trust had tortured him. "José. Can you please show them to their suites?" He pumped his eyebrows. "If you decide to stay, you'll need a place to sleep."

"Thank you," Maddie murmured.

"Of course, mi amigo." José bowed slightly and led the way up the grand staircase.

Maddie took a minute to glance around and appreciate the Spanish architecture. The bold colors and openness of the house fit Brooks' personality. José opened doors across the hallway from each other.

"Thank you," Zack said, then tugged her into one of the rooms and shut the door.

Maddie gazed out at the view of the pool, landscaped gardens, and ocean beyond. It was lovely. If only they could enjoy it.

"You need to trust Brooks," Zack said.

Maddie whipped her head around. His chiseled jaw was firmly set.

He lifted both hands palm up. "I'm not going to reveal your secrets. That's up to you, but I promise you he can protect us, and if you ask, he'll send some men to scout out the harbor, boat docks, and really the entire island to make sure your dad's guys have gone. He has the power, money, and expertise to protect and help us. Wouldn't that make you feel better if you knew where the pirates were?"

The pressure in Maddie's chest released a little bit. "Yes," she admitted.

Zack squeezed her hand. "I know this is hard. You don't know me that well, and Brooks can come on strong, but he's a good guy. I'd trust him with my life. In fact, I have."

"How do you know him?"

Zack grinned but looked a little embarrassed. "I'd tell you the story, but he'll tell it again at dinner, so you'd have to hear it twice." He walked her toward the door. "His version is much better than mine, but don't believe everything he says. He can exaggerate with the best of them."

Zack enjoyed watching Maddie respond to Brooks. He was happy to note that she didn't seem drawn in by his friend. Most women seemed initially attracted to Zack, but once they were around Brooks for five minutes, he had them eating out of the palm of his hand. Sometimes literally. It was gross.

Dinner was laid out on the back patio. The weather was warm with a slight breeze, and the view of the ocean framed by the palm trees was great. But Zack would rather look at Maddie's beautiful face. He knew his friend would hit on her, but it was a risk he'd needed to take when those guys showed up and found them. At least he'd figured out it was the flash drive and gotten rid of it. The impulsive move of putting it in that lady's bag was eating at him. He hoped she hadn't gotten hurt by those idiots.

"So." Maddie looked from Zack to Brooks. "Zack says you're going to tell me the story of how you two met."

"Of course." Brooks set his fork down and took a swallow of his water. "Because he's horrible at stories, and I am amazing."

"Let's not get too overconfident now." Maddie winked at Zack.

"Ha! Confidence is my middle name."

Zack dipped a strip of homemade tortilla into the fresh guacamole and savored the creamy dip. He liked to cook, but it was always a pleasure to eat the food Brooks' cook made.

Brooks rubbed his hands together, his expression full of glee at the opportunity to tell a story. "So, I'm in London for business, and I decide to chase this little trumpet."

Maddie's mouth dropped open. "Excuse me? Did you really just say strumpet? Like, some nineteenth-century hooker?"

"No." Brooks reared back in surprise; then his broad grin appeared. "*Trumpet:* a cute little woman who is too loud but quiets down when she gets some Brooks' attention."

"Oh, my." She glanced at Zack. "Where did you find this guy?"

Zack threw back his head and laughed.

"I'm about to tell you," Brooks said with a wink. "So, I'm chasing this little ... woman through the back streets of London. Having a fun game of cat and mouse."

Maddie glanced from Brooks to Zack. "Is he kidding me right now?" she asked Zack.

"Sadly, no."

"No interrupting the story." Brooks tsked and continued. "I turn the corner into an alleyway and come upon a fight—no, a brawl, really." He gestured to Zack.

Zack couldn't help shifting in his chair. He knew Brooks would tell the story with all of his flair, but he'd never had to endure it while someone he really wanted to impress listened. At first Maddie had been a distraction and an opportunity to help a beautiful woman and do something different, but she was already coming to mean a lot more to him.

"Our world-class Olympian got himself on the wrong side of town. Some thugs decided to rough him up and steal his cash and his pretty diamond earrings."

There it was. How much would Brooks reveal about how the fight affected Zack's Olympics hopes and what a punk he had been? Brooks was the only person who knew the real reason he was there. Well, except for Zack's dad, but he didn't warrant thinking about.

"Diamond earrings?" Maddie asked Zack.

He shrugged his shoulders and ate a bite of pinto beans.

"He was a different man back then, my love. Lots of hair and jewelry," Brooks answered for him. "Not the calm, Zen-like creature who sits here before us."

Zack sputtered and coughed. "Zen-like?"

"He'll give us a yoga demonstration after dinner." Brooks waved a hand. "Anyway. He was taking on four of them and putting up a pretty good fight. I wouldn't have stepped in—a man likes to finish a battle like that on his own—but I recognized Zack from all the media coverage. Who could've missed the article in the *Rising Star*? I didn't want to let those thugs mess up that pretty face for his next magazine shoot or have him miss out on his race the next day."

Zack rolled his eyes and drank some of his margarita. It was tart, just the way he liked it. "Such a champion, aren't you, my friend?"

"Don't you know it? I've been in a few fights in my day." Brooks actually looked a little embarrassed. Zack was tempted to share his friend's secrets, but that wasn't something he would ever do. "Together we took care of them and turned them over to the bobbies. My boy has been eternally in my debt ever since. For payment, he comes to visit and eats my food. Couldn't ask for a better friend." Brooks roared at his own joke.

Maddie smiled at him. Zack returned the smile, but he felt Brooks' devotion to him pretty deeply and couldn't make light of it. "Whatever you want to say, Brooks. You're the best friend I've got."

Brooks nodded slightly, and then said, "Now that is the most pathetic thing I've ever heard. You need to get out more, my boy." He turned to Maddie. "Enough about us. We want to hear about you. How'd you find this boy of mine, and why haven't you ditched him for me yet?"

Maddie choked a little bit on the rice she'd just put in her mouth. Her eyes darted around the open patio.

"We're alone," Brooks assured her. "And even if my staff was around, you could trust them."

Zack nodded in agreement. Maddie met his gaze. She seemed to trust him, but they hadn't known each other very long, and she'd obviously escaped from some very untrustworthy men. This had to be hard.

She swallowed and said quietly, "My father was a pirate."

Brooks' eyebrows dipped down and his face turned serious, which was an odd look for him. "Bad sort of thing to be."

Maddie exhaled slowly. "His assistant, Bello, started an uprising against him. I escaped in a boat and crash-landed on Zack's island." Zack reached over and squeezed her hand. She smiled tremulously at him. "Bello is still after me."

"With how many men, and why is he after you?"

"Eight or—no, there were nine men on the boat. He wanted my ... attention." She studied her plate. "But I think it's really about the papers and flash drive my father gave me. My father instructed me to get them to the American authorities, specifically Homeland Security."

Brooks glanced over her as if she was hiding both the papers and the flash drive. "What is on the flash drive and the papers, and where are they?"

"I don't know what's on them, only that I need to get them to the authorities. Oh, and the bag had passports and money for me." She sighed heavily. "The papers were in a sealed bag, but I lost it when I crashed next to Zack's island. The flash drive must've had a tracking device on it. Zack hid it on a lady who was taking the ferry to the mainland, and Bello's men followed it. That's why we need to get back to Zack's island and find the packet. Hopefully, it's right by where I crashed."

Brooks ran a hand through his hair. He looked from Maddie to Zack, then pursed his lips together. "So, this Bello could still be looking for you on *my* island once he realizes that you ditched the flash drive? It doesn't sound like he'll give up that easily."

Maddie's golden skin seemed to blanch. "Yes," she whispered.

"We need to get moving." Brooks stood and started calling out names and commands. Zack nodded his agreement as Brooks instructed José to go to the yacht club and make sure the boat was stocked with gas, water, and food. There was no reason to take Zack's yacht that the pirates could recognize. A few other men were instructed to go scout Cozumel and see if they could find Bello and his men. Maddie gave them as many names and descriptions of the pirates as she could.

Brooks finished his instructions and sat down. "Now, we wait." He drummed his fingers on the table, ate a few bites, then stood. "I hate waiting."

Zack couldn't help the gut-rumbling laughter that came out. Maddie smiled at him. It felt good after all the stress of the past few hours. He was glad they'd come to Brooks. Maddie's safety was worth the worry over Brooks stealing her.

Maddie suppressed a laugh at Brooks' nervous energy as he paced the patio and threw out questions to her. She quickly forgot her mirth as the seriousness of the situation pressed down on her. Thank heavens for Zack and Brooks' willingness to help. Once again, a man she barely knew was turning his life upside down to protect her.

She blinked back a few tears. She'd never been a crier and was hard pressed to think of times when she'd wanted to sit down and bawl, but this was all pretty overwhelming.

"Did you get enough to eat?" Brooks gestured to her near-empty plate.

"Yes, thank you, it was wonderful."

"Good, good. Let's go into my office and plan." He gestured to the doorway. Zack took Maddie's hand, and Brooks followed them through the main floor, their feet tapping on the slate flooring.

As they settled into his plush office chairs, Maddie couldn't help but gush out, "You two are doing so much for me. I don't know how I'll ever repay you."

"Just don't cry." Brooks pulled a face. "We never know how to deal with a crying woman. And give us lots of kisses of gratitude."

Zack emitted a low growl. His hand tightened over hers. "She'll be giving me all the kisses of gratitude."

Maddie quivered at the thought.

"You're going to be in even more debt to me, then." Brooks winked at Maddie.

"Me in debt to you or Zack in debt to you?" Maddie asked.

"Zack. If you're not willing to kiss me, there's nothing else I want from you."

Maddie wasn't sure if she should be offended. "I didn't say I wasn't willing to kiss you."

"Oh?" Brooks' eyebrows arched up.

Zack wrapped his arm around Maddie and pulled her closer. "Believe me; you don't want to kiss him."

Maddie glanced into his dark eyes and gave her best innocent expression. "Why not?"

"Because I'm a much better kisser." To prove his point, he captured her lips with his own while Brooks hollered in the background. Maddie couldn't hear a thing Brooks said as Zack's arms and smell surrounded her, and his kisses took away all the stress and worry of the past day. He finally pulled back, grinning at her.

"Okay, that's enough of *that* garbage," Brooks harrumphed. "Kissing in front of me when I've got no woman to give me comfort. Here I am, this perfect specimen, and I've been bested by my little bro."

Maddie laughed and leaned against Zack's chest. She'd take kissing Zack as payment for their help any day. She didn't want to kiss Brooks, yet Maddie couldn't help but like him. He was over the top, but he was genuine. He seemed to want to shock her, but he wasn't leering at her like Bello and his men did.

"Are you a bodybuilder?" she asked Brooks, referring to his comment of being the perfect specimen.

Zack and Brooks exchanged a look, and Brooks laughed. "She likes my physique more than yours, little bro," Brooks insisted.

"No, actually, I like Zack's better. Yours is too … much." Everything about Brooks was too much, but he was growing on her. She liked laughing, and he definitely made her laugh, but Zack was more attractive and intriguing to her.

Zack released one arm from her waist and flexed. "Move aside. She likes me better."

"I should hope so. She is your woman."

"I wish," Zack said.

Maddie's gaze widened. She wasn't even close to being Zack's woman. Besides the few kisses they'd shared, they had no kind of relationship. She hardly knew him, and after they made it to America, she probably wouldn't see him again. The thought saddened her.

Brooks' phone rang. He listened for a second, gave a few more commands, and hung up. "Let's go. They're ready for us."

They hurried out the front doors and loaded into a black Hummer. A driver dropped them off at the same yacht club where Zack's boat was moored. Maddie was edgy, searching everywhere for signs of Bello or his men. If they'd returned from following the ferry, and that poor woman who had the flash drive in her bag, they could be anywhere, and she thought the place to house yachts would be their first stop.

A young man escorted them up a ramp and onto a beautiful yacht. It was larger than Zack's, but not as big as her father's. Brooks thanked all his men, palmed them each some money, and rushed them off the boat. Maddie was semi-surprised that he didn't keep some of them around to serve him. He seemed to like people serving him.

He settled into the captain's chair, and Maddie and Zack sat down on a cushioned bench next to him. Maddie searched the boat docks behind them, but no one was running after them in pursuit. As Brooks maneuvered the boat out into the ocean and increased the speed, she finally felt her shoulders lower and her hands unclench. Bello hadn't found her.

"Just the three of us?" she asked.

"Yes. Zack can spell off piloting with me and cooking us food." Brooks winked at her.

"I can also drive," she offered.

"You don't drive a yacht like this, love; you pilot it."

Maddie nodded. Her father had probably told her that.

"No cooking for you?" Brooks laughed.

"I make a mean Ramen noodle."

"That's why you like him, because he can cook?" Brooks gestured to Zack. "I can order people to cook delicacies that make Zack's meals look like dog food."

Zack glanced at her. Maddie smiled shyly at him, not sure how to tell Brooks Zack's cooking ability was not why she was drawn to him. "This is a beautiful boat."

"You like my little Ferretti, eh? It's not as fast as Zack's Butterfly, but every bit as luxurious, and I've done a few modifications to up the speed."

Maddie had been around boys who bragged about how fast their car could go or how big their truck tires were, but she was completely out of her element with these two men, who had to be millionaires, or maybe even billionaires, with no one but themselves to spend it on. Zack was quite different from Brooks, though. He didn't brag. He was simply himself, and that was more than enough.

Zack squeezed her arm. "Do you want to go lie down for a little while and take a nap? It'll take us about four hours to get back home, and then almost twenty-four hours to get to Key West."

Maddie swallowed, her heart thumping faster. Was Zack suggesting she lie down by herself or with him? Rather than try to clarify, she said, "I'm okay. You can go rest if you want."

He shook his head, his eyes cutting to his friend. "I'm not leaving you alone with him."

"He doesn't want to risk me stealing you away with all this charm." Brooks gestured to himself and winked.

"Lucky for Zack, I find you hilarious but not one bit charming."

Zack was the one laughing now as Brooks feigned a pain in his chest. "That was vicious. If I'm not impressive to you, I will just stop talking and become a chauffeur."

"I don't think you could stop talking," Maddie challenged with a raised eyebrow.

Zack squeezed her arm. "No way he could. Can you imagine Brooks taking a vow of silence?"

"I could," Brooks insisted.

"Ha. You've already failed." The small island of Cozumel fell behind them with no sign of any yachts following. Maddie relaxed even further, feeling light and happy and safe with Zack and Brooks.

"That wasn't a fair contest. I will start my vow of silence ... now!" Brooks focused on steering the yacht and wouldn't look at the two of them.

"Oh, this is going to be nice," Zack said. He leaned against the cushions and closed his eyes. "I'll just take a nap and enjoy the quiet."

"No." Maddie inclined close to his side and put her feet up. Her eyes felt heavy too. "We have to tempt him into talking."

Brooks shook his head. His mouth was set in a tight line.

"Not sure if I want to do that." Zack leaned close to her and his lips brushed along her forehead.

Maddie shivered from his touch. She inched a bit closer. Zack lifted his arm and wrapped it around her shoulder. She leaned into him and glanced up at his handsome face. "You can tell me all about him while he takes his vow of silence. Why does he live in Cozumel when he's obviously American? How did he become so full of himself?"

Brooks smirked but didn't take the bait.

"Oh, the first one's easy," Zack said. "He hides away in Cozumel because he was sick of being rejected by all the women in California."

"I have never been rejected by a woman," Brooks spit out.

They both started laughing.

Brooks smiled and shook his head. "So I'm not very good at silence, and besides Maddie here, I am *rarely* rejected by women."

"Rarely?" Zack shook his head. "I think we define that word differently, my friend."

Maddie listened to them tease each other. Feeling content and safe in Zack's arms, she let her eyes drift closed a few times. What seemed like minutes later, Zack sat up and it startled her. He held on to her and helped her stand. Her legs felt a little wobbly.

"Good thing that I'm here, or you two would've just slept the trip away and ended up who knows where?" Brooks teased from the captain's chair.

"Where are we?" Maddie asked, stifling a yawn. The ocean was dark around them. How long had she slept?

"Home." Zack squeezed her waist, then released her and pointed out the front windows.

The lights of his island glowed like a welcoming beacon. Maddie's heart leapt at the thought of home, a home with Zack. No, that was crazy. Her next thought was fear. "What if Bello left some men here?"

Zack actually laughed like he didn't have a fear in the world and pointed at Brooks. "That's why we brought him along."

Zack took the wheel from Brooks, who rushed down below. He

returned several minutes later with a large rifle thing and a pistol, strapping a knife onto his leg. Maddie instinctively backed away.

"He tells the story of how we met wrong," Zack said. "He saved me single-handedly. He's an expert in hand-to-hand combat, but he's not bad with a semi-automatic either."

"Or a pistol, knife, sniper's rifle, and I've been known to hold my own with sabers as well." Brooks flashed her his now-familiar overconfident smile.

Maddie was glad Brooks was on their side. "Who trained you in all of that?"

"That is a story for late at night when I'm feeling nostalgic, stupid, and someone's slipped something in my drink." He shot a glance at Zack.

Zack held up his hands. "Wasn't me."

Maddie found herself laughing at the two of them, despite the pressure of fear that Bello or his men might've stayed here or come back. If she had a brother, she imagined he would've been similar to Brooks, and she would've loved him. She glanced at Zack. No brotherly feelings for that man; she was all tied up in too much tingle and heat to want to be any blood relation.

Zack guided the boat into his harbor, and Brooks jumped off and secured the lines. "You two sleepyheads stay here and smooch a little more. I'll be back when I have the all-clear."

"What if you don't come back?" Maddie couldn't help but say it, the words almost choking her with concern for him and for them if they didn't have Brooks protecting them.

"Then you sail your butts out of here, go get my men, and come back with an army." He grinned. "Don't worry, little one. I'll come back." He jogged down the dock, stopping to tap in a code on the door Maddie and Zack had used to escape. Had that only been this morning? It felt like a lifetime.

Maddie glanced at Zack. He turned off the motor, which had cooled down, and got off to check the lines. He came back a few seconds later, took one look at her face, and opened his arms. She fell against him. "I feel like we should go with him," she said.

"I know, but I've learned to trust him." He chuckled. "I made the mistake of trailing him once and almost cost us both our lives. You know what he told me?"

She shook her head against his solid chest.

"He said—" Zack mimicked Brooks' lilting tones: "'You are a runner and a cook. When I need either of those things, I will invite you along. Don't bug me when I'm fighting. I fight alone.'" He laughed softly. "He really will be okay. He's a one-man ninja team with lots of weapons."

Time ticked by slowly as Zack watched the dock, and Maddie listened intently for any kind of disturbance. She had no clue how much later, Brooks appeared out of the dark at the other end of the dock. He jogged toward them, grinning. "Nobody home to greet me. What a bummer."

Maddie sighed. Thank heavens. They waited while Brooks grabbed a few things, then walked up the steps and entered the house through the back patio. It felt so good to be here.

Brooks thumped Zack on the back. "Now, you slept the evening away while I got us here safe. I'm going to set up the command center and alarms. You take first watch, and I'll try to sleep." He glanced at his watch. "Wake me up at three a.m., and then you can get a few hours in before we find this packet and set sail again."

Zack nodded. "Sounds like a plan."

"What's the command center?" Maddie asked.

Brooks' eyes lit up. "Only the greatest room ever built into a house."

"The man who built this house was a bit paranoid," Zack added.

"Paranoid!" Brooks interrupted. "Smart, my friend. Brilliant. A visionary! Don't disgrace his ingenuity by undermining it. You can never be too cautious."

Zack inclined his head to Brooks and pumped his eyebrows at his friend. "The man who built this house was a visionary. He installed cameras and sensors all around the island with a room for monitoring them. If everything is turned on, we'll have an alert every time a dolphin surfaces or a larger-than-normal wave breaks. It's more than a little annoying. I never turn it on unless Brooks is here."

"It's a beautiful thing." Brooks sighed, a grin on his face.

Maddie laughed, but was reassured that they would know if the pirates were coming. "What should I do to help?"

Brooks' eyes travelled over her. "You could come snuggle me to help me sleep ..."

"Brooks," Zack warned.

Maddie shook her head. "In your unfulfilled fantasies."

Brooks chuckled. "Ah, no. I was afraid that would be your answer. You can keep my boy company or get some more sleep yourself. Au revoir."

He carried his weapons and bag off down the hallway.

Zack rolled his eyes. "I used to apologize for him, but we've been friends too long. I hope he doesn't offend you."

"No. Feels like an annoying older brother."

Zack smiled. "Good. Do you want to go rest?"

"I don't think I could sleep after that nap. I'll sit up with you."

Zack fidgeted with his hands for a minute. The air hung with an awkwardness that hadn't been between them since they'd met. They had hours to kill until daylight, when they could look for the package, and Maddie didn't know what they'd do with all that time. She wouldn't mind snuggling like they'd done on Brooks' boat and talking the hours away, but Zack seemed uncomfortable. Had she been acting too familiar with him, and now he wanted to slow things down? He'd told her that he didn't like women coming on to him. She hated the thought of reversing the level of intimacy they'd found in the past day, but she didn't want to make Zack feel pressured to hold her or assume they had a relationship when they didn't.

He gestured toward the couches. "Sit, please. Or you're welcome to use the room you had last night if you want to sleep or shower, or whatever." He looked away. "If you'll excuse me, I'll be right back."

Maddie watched him go, then went to her suite and used the bathroom, brushed her teeth, and tried to improve her appearance a little bit. What she wouldn't give for some lipstick.

She wandered back into the living room, but Zack wasn't there yet. Taking her time, she looked at the pictures on the shelves. She'd guess his mom, sister, brother-in-law, and niece were in most of them. His mom was a stately blonde, maybe of Scandinavian descent. His sister was a beautiful version of Zack with lots of black curly hair and a refined, gorgeous face. Her husband was tall and redheaded, a great contrast to Zack and the sister's milk-chocolate skin. The niece was absolutely adorable. Tons of dark hair curled around her pixie face. Her eyes sparkled with mischief and intelligence in every picture with her parents. Those same eyes seemed wizened and sad in more recent pictures. How did a child deal with losing both parents? Maddie had just lost one parent, who she'd never been close to, and it still felt a little tender.

Zack entered the room. He smelled really nice and fresh, like he'd showered. "Brooks will probably beat me for slacking on the lookout job, but I really needed a shower and the surveillance equipment does a great job. Brooks checks it every time he visits."

"I thought you smelled yummy already." Maddie bit her lip and glanced away.

Zack took a few steps closer. "Are you hungry, thirsty?"

Thirsty for your kiss. "Water would be great." She smiled to herself.

He got them each a glass of water and then motioned to the couches. "Do you want to sit?"

Maddie hated that it'd gotten awkward between them. Had she overstepped boundaries snuggling him on the ride back or said something with Brooks that had turned him off from her? Maybe he was sick of his life being in upheaval for a woman he barely knew.

She sank into the couch in the living room, enjoying the cool water sliding past her lips and down her throat. Setting her glass on a side table, she laced her hands together. "And now we wait."

Zack nodded. "Luckily we're both a little more patient than Brooks."

Maddie laughed. "So you met him in London, and, after he fought for you, it was instant friendship?"

"He came to London in 2012 and was the only one who wanted to be seen with me after the debacle. When I returned home to New York, things were ... uncomfortable for me." He cleared his throat and looked away. "So I went to visit Brooks in Cozumel. He helped me find this island."

Maddie swallowed at the pain on his face. "Were people rude to you after the Olympics?"

He shrugged. "Not rude. It was more ... I don't know, disappointed. Awkward."

She clasped her hands together and asked something she probably shouldn't. "What happened?"

His head whipped up. "What do you mean?"

"You'd never made a mistake before. I remember all the hype about it." She looked down. "I used to trip all the time, but I've worked really hard to be coordinated. I thought maybe we were kindred spirits until I read up about how you'd never tripped, always smooth and in control."

"I like how you work so hard to be fit and coordinated."

Maddie blushed. "Thank you." They sat in silence for a few moments. "Now I've revealed my awkwardness to you. Your turn."

Zack circled his glass with his hand, rubbing away the condensation with his thumb. "Please don't share this with anyone."

Maddie leaned slightly forward, much too interested, because Zack was willing to share something with her that not many people knew.

"I was injured in the fight the night before. My ankle got twisted. It was just a sprain, but it was enough to affect my performance." He stared directly at her. "Only Brooks and one of my coaches know the truth about it."

Maddie shook her head. "But why? Why didn't you tell the world? Everyone blamed you instead of understanding."

"If I told the world about the fight, you know they'd demand to know why I was in that fight in the first place. I've been on my share of morning talk shows. I know how they are." His eyes darkened. He set the glass down on the side table and clasped his hands together. Tense seconds passed. Finally, he said, "Well, aren't you going to ask why I was in that fight?"

"Um." Maddie chewed at her cheek. She wanted to know, but was it her right? He'd already shared so much with her. "If you want to tell me."

He stood and paced the room, looking out at the dark night

instead of at her. "My father and I fought for years over 'my silly running obsession,' as he called it."

"Silly!" Maddie exclaimed. "You were the best in the world."

He nodded his thanks before continuing, "We never got along—both too hardheaded, my sister would say—but my Olympic dreams made it even worse. Especially because my mom supported me in it. As a teenager, he forced me to work long hours for him when I should've been training. I actually liked the work and excelled at it, but being an Olympian was my dream. My mom hired the best trainers, and they worked with me whenever I had a spare minute. I'd go to the gym at five a.m. and train until school started at seven-thirty." He smiled. "Dad never knew."

Maddie stayed silent, watching him pace and talk.

"My dad's mistake was paying me too well and teaching me too much. By the time I graduated college, I had a huge portfolio of investments that were doing so well I could pursue my dream without any support from him. My mom continued to hire trainers and travel with me; I think just to show that she supported me."

Maddie was fully invested in his story, but not sure how it led to his fight. "Your parents are still together?"

"Oh, yeah. They love each other. My dad adores my mom, and she has no clue about ... what he did."

"The fight?" she guessed.

"Yep." He clenched and unclenched his fist. "I was just leaving a team dinner and went for a walk to stretch my legs. Those guys grabbed me and hauled me into a van, took me to the alley where Brooks found me. I thought they were going to try to get ransom or something. They never said a word, just started beating on me."

As horrible as Maddie's father was, he'd never hurt her directly or on purpose. "How'd you know it was your dad?"

"I wouldn't have if Brooks hadn't shown up and turned the fight around." Zack gave her an embarrassed smile. "He beat the truth out of one of them. They claimed a tall black man who looked a lot like me but with darker skin had paid them to ambush me so I'd be forced to quit competing."

"Wow." Maddie reclined into the cushions and mulled it all over.

Zack settled next to her, though his fists were still clenched. "You weren't just running from the women and the Olympics disaster when you came here?"

Zack met her gaze. "No."

"Do you and your dad talk now?"

He shrugged. "We had it out after my sister's funeral. He tried to guilt me into coming back to work for him, worried about me wasting all my talent. The only talent he's ever thought I had was with business and marketing. I told him I knew he orchestrated the attack. He fully admitted to it, but claimed the idiots were supposed to rough me up *after* my Olympic performance. Then I'd get my chance to shine but would for sure retire, having just finished an Olympics. He wanted them to rough me up enough so I wouldn't be healthy enough to continue training, and he hoped while I recovered I'd fall in love with working with him again and never go back to running competitively. He apologized for the mistake." Zack let out a loud breath and shook his head. "But of course, he claimed it was in my best interest, and I needed to forget about it and move on."

Maddie's hand covered her mouth. "He wanted them to hurt you bad enough you couldn't train?" she repeated. "Wow. Here I thought having a pirate for a father was bad."

Zack gave a surprised laugh. "We both lucked out in the father department, eh?"

"Seems like it. So you don't see him at all?"

"We came to a truce. I wouldn't reveal to my mom what he'd done, and he wouldn't keep Chalise from me. It works for us."

Maddie's heart went out to him. She still wondered why her father had put her in danger. Zack's father had him beat up so he couldn't fulfill his dream. Crazy.

"Now you know all my dirt; tell me about yourself."

Maddie smiled at him. She'd kissed this man a few times, but they really didn't know each other very well. "Well, besides this adventure, I'm just a regular girl from the metropolis of Bozeman, Montana." She gave the name her best hick-lilt, and Zack rewarded her with a smile. "Lived with my mom until I graduated from high school. Then I got my own apartment with some close friends and spent the past six years at Montana State studying, playing volleyball, and enjoying college."

"And now you're graduated and ready to take on the world."

"That's right." She felt sad for Zack. In a way, his father was right. He'd had unreal talent in hurdles and running and what sounded like a brilliant business mind, and he was just enjoying life on this island. She knew that a lot of people would say he was living the dream, but the vacation life would get boring after a while, especially for someone as smart and talented as Zack.

"What's your degree in?" he asked.

"Speech pathology, with a focus on early intervention and preschool-aged children."

"Really?" He studied her intently, opened his mouth, and then closed it. Finally, he said, "That's great. You must love children."

"For sure. They're so funny, and they love me no matter if I'm having a bad hair day or don't have on makeup."

"You don't have on makeup right now and you look fabulous."

"Thanks," she murmured.

The silence sat between them for a few seconds. Then Zack said, "My niece is like that, always hugging me, but she can't talk, so ..."

"Her speech is delayed?" Maddie asked carefully, not wanting to pry.

"Way past delayed. They don't know when she'll talk, if ever. Nobody can come up with the right term for it. They don't know if she's just slow or if the trauma of her parents dying when she was two messed her up."

Maddie glanced at a picture of Zack hugging Chalise on the side table. "There's too much intelligence in her eyes. She's definitely not slow."

Zack leaned toward her. "That's what I say. My mom and dad have her in all these special programs and with all these therapists, but I think she needs a break. I keep begging them to let me keep her for a few months. I think she just needs love and understanding. No one pushing her to talk."

"I think that's a great plan." It might not be a by-the-book plan, but in a trauma situation, the book sometimes had to go out the window. Zack was so full of love and patience, she almost wondered if he was too good to be true.

Zack smiled at her, and they sat without saying anything for a few seconds. Then he took a deep breath and said, "I'm sorry that I implied with Brooks earlier today that we were a couple or something."

He was going there? Well, that stank. Why had he kissed her repeatedly if he didn't want to be with her? He was probably just enjoying a fling. She'd be gone in another day. She swallowed and could hardly trust her voice. "You're sorry?"

"I was trying to protect you from Brooks. He's a huge player and ... I mean, I love him like a brother, but I didn't want you to fall for him or him to try his tricky charm on you or ..." He rubbed his shaved head with his palm. "This is not coming out right."

Maddie wasn't sure whether to be hurt or flattered. "You were trying to protect me from your friend?"

He nodded.

Maddie's eyes narrowed. She knew she shouldn't say what she was thinking, but she couldn't hold it in. "So to protect me from your friend, you kissed me on the *way* to his house this morning, on your yacht when we got to Cozumel, and a third time when Bello's men were closing in on us? I hadn't even met Brooks when you kissed me those times."

"Oh, um, well, I wasn't thinking very clearly, and I guess ..." Zack's eyes met hers; then he focused out the picture windows. "I don't want *anyone* to take advantage of you."

"What if I wanted you to take advantage of me?" Maddie's face felt hot. That had *not* come out the way she intended. Far too bold.

Zack's dark skin broke into a grin of white teeth. "Are you serious?"

"Well, not take advantage, but I sure wouldn't complain about getting to know you better and maybe a few more kisses." She was being really forward. This wasn't like her, but then again, maybe it was. She'd never had a man she was interested in like this before. The boys she'd dated in college were no match for Zack in any capacity.

Zack scooted closer on the sofa. He gently took her hand. "Maddie." His tongue darted over his lips, and she couldn't help but focus on his well-formed mouth. "Before the Olympics, I dated a lot and—" He swallowed. "—got burned by women who were only after my money or my status as America's Most Beautiful Man."

He studied her, and Maddie wanted to tell him she was interested in him for him; she couldn't care less about the money or his looks ... okay, his looks were really nice, but not for the status of it.

"But I'd really like to get to know you better, see where this leads."

"Hmm. I don't know."

"You don't know?" His eyes widened and he leaned back.

"It's all depends." Maddie tilted her head to the side and batted her lashes.

"On what?" His forehead wrinkled.

"If kissing is going to be included." Her stomach smoldered from the idea, and the embers burned into a roaring fire when he grinned and pulled her closer.

"There is definitely going to be kissing."

Zack lowered his head to hers and took possession of her mouth. Maddie turned into his arms. He lifted her off the couch and onto his lap. She pressed against his muscled chest, enjoying each motion of his lips and his hands.

"Holy brother of the Buddha!" Brooks' voice was loud enough that it came right through the romantic moment, ripping them apart.

Maddie slid onto her own couch cushion and looked guiltily at Zack. He laughed and stroked her arm. "What do you want, Brooks?"

"What do I want? You to actually act like a proper sentry. The pirates could've sailed into the port and be circling the house, and you two wouldn't have a clue until your heads were severed from your shoulders!" Brooks blustered around in front of them, gesturing angrily to the dark world outside.

"The alarms would've sounded. Besides, we haven't been kissing that long." Zack leaned into Maddie, and they exchanged a glance. "Not nearly long enough."

"I've been watching you make out for ten minutes."

Maddie's entire face was on fire. Hopefully her dark skin would hide any blush from the men.

"Liar," Zack said drily. "You barely walked in here."

"How do you know?"

"You couldn't keep quiet for ten seconds, much less ten minutes."

Maddie laughed, but she was suddenly exhausted, and she knew she couldn't keep up with Brooks' banter or energy much longer. She tugged away from Zack's hold and stood. Her body felt empty without him next to her. The sad expression on his face almost had her jumping back into his arms, even with Brooks watching. "I'm going to go lie down for a little bit."

Zack nodded. "Good idea." He stood.

"Don't even think about it, lover lips." Brooks folded his arms across his chest, his large biceps bulging. "You're going to stay up with me, watch for the pirates, and bake me a cheesecake."

"Cheesecake?" Maddie couldn't help but laugh.

"No one can make it like Zack." Brooks winked at her.

Zack shook his head. "I'll just walk her to her room, then be right back to deal with you."

Brooks held up his hands and let them pass. "As long as there's cheesecake. I might save you some," he called after Maddie, "*if* you share those lips with everyone in the house."

Maddie laughed. "Never been a cheesecake fan," she called back. Brooks' deep chuckle followed them down the hall.

They reached her room and stopped outside the door. Zack traced his thumb down her cheek. "I'm making the cheesecake; you can have as much as you like."

Maddie giggled. "You could tell I was lying to him, then? I adore cheesecake."

"I'm just glad you don't want to kiss him."

"Only you." She gazed up at him, impressed with her boldness. If she ever saw her friends again, she'd have a lot of great stories.

Zack lowered his head and kissed her gently. Maddie wrapped her arms around his neck and lifted herself on tiptoes. He deepened the kiss, and they were in their own world when Brooks bellow interrupted. "Enough of this mac-daddying. Get in here and bake, boy!"

Maddie fell back onto her heels, feeling a little unsteady. Zack released her and nodded at the bed. "I hope you can sleep."

"With two big old studs watching out for me, I can."

"I'm the only stud here."

"Guess I can agree with that."

Zack traced a hand down her face and then backed up a step. Maddie smiled and walked to the bathroom. All of her worries over Zack being annoyed that she'd shown up on his island and him being forced to help her were unfounded. He wanted to be with her. She wished for a cell phone to scream her joy to one of her friends.

She was still smiling when she lay down to sleep ten minutes later. Her smile grew when she heard Brooks' loud protests. "I am not jealous! The woman must be thickheaded to want you instead of me."

Maddie burrowed into the soft bed and didn't care if she was thickheaded. Zack was more of a man than she'd ever dreamed of being with, and he seemed to want to be with her as much as she wanted him.

CHAPTER SEVEN

M addie's eyes popped open as her room lightened with the rising sun. She jumped out of bed and hurriedly showered, brushed her hair, and got dressed in the same red-and-white-striped sundress Zack had bought her. It fit her better than his sister's clothes, and he'd seemed to like it on her. She smiled, thinking of the appreciative look in his eyes. He seemed to *really* like it on her.

She was excited to see Zack again this morning, and anxious to find the packet of papers from her father. Would she finally know why her father had never had time for her? Maybe there was something in the papers that would exonerate him in her eyes. A girl could hope.

Rushing down the hallway, she stopped short when she entered the great room. Zack and Brooks were each on a couch, sprawled out and sleeping like the dead. She laughed. Glancing around at the ocean, she was relieved not to see any sign of her father's yacht. She didn't think Bello would come back here, but who knew?

She walked into the kitchen, found some pancake mix and eggs, and started cooking. The cheesecake in the fridge looked fabulous. She let herself have a small bite of the swirled orange-and-white cake. Mango. Yum. Zack was going to have to share that recipe.

Grabbing a pan and metal ladle, she banged them together several times, giggling to herself. Zack sat upright, then swayed back down into the cushions. Brooks grabbed his head. "What's with all the racket, woman?"

"Breakfast," she said sweetly.

"I don't know if I can ever eat again. Never gorge on cheesecake and then sleep on a stinking couch," Brooks growled.

"I'm blaming you," Zack said. "I told you it needed at least twelve hours to set up properly."

Maddie laughed at the two of them stretching and looking beat up from the bad night's sleep. "Go shower quick so we can eat and find my packet."

"Wow." Brooks' eyebrows shot up. "Kiss her nonstop and she becomes a demanding, noisy diva. I think you should cease and desist, my man."

"Not a chance." Zack grinned at her.

Maddie laughed and turned back to flip the pancakes. "Shower. Now."

Zack chuckled and Brooks grumbled all the way out of the room. A few minutes later they were both back to scarf down the simple breakfast she'd made and some of the exotic fruit she'd cut up. "Do you go into Belize for supplies?" Maddie asked Zack.

He nodded. "But I grow a lot of produce right here."

"Impressive."

Zack pumped his eyebrows. "That's not the only impressive thing about me."

"I know that."

"Enough of this garbage." Brooks shoved back from the counter and took his plate to the sink. "Do we need scuba gear to find this package or just masks and snorkels?"

"I think we'll be okay with masks and snorkels." Zack squeezed her hand but focused on his friend.

Maddie had only eaten a few bites of eggs and pancakes, but she didn't have much of an appetite. The worry over finding the packet, what might be in the packet, and Bello coming after them again was wearing on her. Standing, she started cleaning up the kitchen. It only took a few minutes with all of them working together, and then the men changed into swimming suits and T-shirts and met her by the patio door. Maddie wished she had a swimming suit and could join them, but Zack had reassured her last night that they were both accomplished divers and could take care of it.

"Not sure why I listened to the queen bee and showered just to go jump in the salt water for her." Brooks rolled his eyes.

Zack laughed. "The shower helped me feel human again."

"You'd agree with her if she told you to become a monk."

Zack's eyebrows lifted. "What religion do you belong to, Maddie? I can convert."

She shook her head, laughing. They walked past the pool and garden area, grabbing masks and snorkels from a storage container by the pool. Maddie tripped on the smooth concrete, and Zack was right there to steady her. She smiled her appreciation.

As they walked down the stairs, through the sand, and to the end of the dock, Maddie savored this beautiful spot of earth. It was like something out of a travel brochure. Palm trees waved in the breeze, a sandy beach stretched around the island, and the water was bright blue and so clear under the dock she could see tropical fish swimming around.

Zack sat on the edge of the dock and peeled off his T-shirt. She forgot all about the view around her, taking in nicely built pecs and shoulders and his hollowed-out, sculpted abdomen. A low whistle came out of her mouth before she clamped her hand over it. Zack glanced up at her with a grin. My, oh my, no one could argue with the *Rising Star* for claiming he was the Most Beautiful Man in America, and she had a hard time finding fault with any woman who chased him—though she wanted to have the right to tell all those other women to back off so she could have him all to herself.

Brooks moved in front of her view of Zack and peeled off his shirt, leaning forward and flexing his chest and arms. He was bulkier than Zack, and each muscle was defined like a competitive bodybuilder. Still no match to Zack in her eyes. Maddie pushed at him. "You're blocking the view."

Zack chuckled, and Brooks' jaw dropped. "You have to be the

densest female I have ever encountered." He dropped his shirt and sat next to Zack.

They rubbed some drops of anti-fog onto their goggle lenses and then rinsed them in the salt water. Placing the masks over their eyes, they fell to the side of the dock and swam away from her toward the wreck. All levity evaporated as Maddie watched them go. She scanned the ocean, relieved not to see a white yacht cruising toward them.

Brooks and Zack had already reached the listing boat when she focused in on them again. Brooks inspected the boat while Zack swam around. Zack surfaced and said something to Brooks, then dove deeper. Maddie's hands clenched together. The seconds slowed down as she waited, praying. If they didn't find that package, what would she do? Run from Bello the rest of her life?

Zack resurfaced and shook his head. Disappointment swirled through her. Maddie squinted against the bright sunlight glinting off the gently rolling waves. Zack and Brooks swam around for a few more minutes while she paced the dock and gnawed on her thumbnail. She prayed for help. At home, she'd been active in her church her entire life, but she'd never needed help from above like this. Zack and Brooks continued diving and surfacing, but came up empty each time.

Zack was moving in a semicircle out from the wreck, toward the beach. The water was shallower where he was. Maddie held her breath every time he lifted something out of the water, but the packet seemed to be gone. Had Bello found it? Was it buried in the sand?

Zack straightened up in water about to his chest and held up the packet.

Maddie whooped with joy. "Yes! You found it!" She barely restrained herself from jumping in the water and swimming to him.

Brooks glanced up and then swam over to the dock. Zack headed for the beach. Maddie ran to meet him. It took him a few more seconds to get out of the water as she waited impatiently. Zack handed the package to her, his goggles resting on his forehead. Maddie clutched the package and flung herself into Zack's arms, kissing him thoroughly and knocking off his goggles. He tasted of salt water, and she loved the feel of his bare back under her fingertips.

"Do you think we should see what's in the sealed documents or just smooch all day?" Brooks asked behind them.

Maddie pulled back. Her eyes flickered over Zack's chest, then back up to his handsome face. "I'd say smooch."

Zack chuckled, then kissed her again.

Brooks stole the package from her hands and stomped through the sand. "I'll just deal with the hard issues by myself, then."

Maddie didn't like having the package out of her hands. She rushed after Brooks. "Give that back."

Brooks held it over his head and grinned wickedly. "For a kiss."

Maddie slugged him in the stomach. His eyes narrowed, but he didn't even flinch.

"Nope, try again." He smirked at her. "My lips are a bit higher."

Maddie tossed her hair and pinned him with a vicious look, though she thought his antics were kind of funny. "I'll smack you in the mouth if you want."

Zack barreled into Brooks and tackled him into the sand. Brooks howled in surprise, and Maddie stole the packet from his hand. The men rolled around in the sand like monkeys, laughing and grunting. Maddie jumped out of their way and headed for the stairs, calling back over her shoulder, "I think you two need another shower."

Zack released Brooks and popped up to his feet. He offered Brooks a hand up. "Stop trying to kiss my woman."

"And here I share everything with you," Brooks grumbled.

Zack slapped him on the back. "You've always been a better friend than I have."

"Don't you forget it."

Maddie smiled slightly at their banter, but she wanted to know what was in this packet too much to contribute. As soon as she got to the pool deck, she sat down at a patio table and tried to rip the packet open. The plastic was thick. She dug a fingernail into it. Zack and Brooks arrived, set their snorkeling gear in the bucket, and peered over her shoulder.

"Here." Brooks pulled a pocketknife from his swimsuit pocket and handed it to her.

"You just happen to have a knife on you?" Maddie blinked up at him.

"He always has a knife on him," Zack corrected.

"He can't always." Zack's friend was the most interesting man she had ever met. She enjoyed being around him, but everything about him was so extreme.

"Honestly, he does."

"What about when you go to America?" Maddie swung her gaze to Brooks. "Don't they take it at customs?"

"Who would ever want to go to there?" Brooks asked, arching one eyebrow, wet sand smeared across his cheek from wrestling with Zack.

Zack chuckled.

"I like America," Maddie muttered. She ignored Brooks, carefully sliced the plastic, and pulled the contents out of the package. There was a bundle of cash—mostly hundred-dollar bills, but also some thousand-peso notes and some hundreds with a queen-looking lady and "Central Bank of Belize" stamped on them. A few passports also dropped out, along with social security cards and birth certificates, with her and her mother's pictures and different names on each set of documents. A fat envelope with her name on it was the last item.

Brooks whistled low. "Wow. Someone thought you needed to disappear."

"Yeah." Maddie wondered if it was wise to have Brooks know everything, but she felt like she could trust both of these men. She glanced up at Zack.

He placed a hand on her shoulder and gave it a soft squeeze. "Do you want me to open it?" He indicated the letter.

The thought hadn't even crossed her mind. Somehow this man not only protected her when she asked for it, he also anticipated what she needed and put her first. He didn't even have to think about it; protecting her seemed instinctive.

It would be hard to read anything from her father, especially with the danger he'd put her in over the last thirty-six hours. The disappointment was familiar, but there was something new—she detested him for failing so miserably. Zack had done more to stand up for her in a day and a half than her father had done in two and a half decades combined. While she felt deeply blessed and grateful for her current situation, realizing what she had missed out on from the one who should have been watching out for her made her shoulders round over and her stomach squirm. If her father were here in front of her, she didn't know whether she'd yell at him or just haul off and punch him.

"Maddie?" said Zack gently.

Maddie cleared her throat and shook her head. With trembling fingers, she peeled the sealed envelope open. She shuffled through the papers quickly. One sheet was addressed to her, while the rest of them were stapled together and said "Homeland Security."

She read the letter aloud, her voice somewhat unsteady.

Dear Madeline,

I've entrusted these documents to you because I know you can clear mine and Bello's names and help us bring down the largest ring of pirates the Caribbean has seen in centuries. I apologize for using you to get the information into the right hands, but I needed someone I could trust and I knew this would be my last opportunity to spend time with you before I died. I'll die happy knowing that you, your mother, and Bello are taken care of.

I haven't been much of a father to you, and I'm sorry about that. At the bottom of this letter, I will include bank institutions and account numbers for your inheritance. My letter to Homeland Security gives them access to the accounts I accumulated illegally. The money I'm leaving you is clean, and even someone as righteous as you should have no qualms using it.

I know money doesn't make up for my lack of time in your life, but I also know you will spend the millions making the world a better place. Your mother and I are both very proud of you, my love. Every time we were together, she would brag about you. You care for others, and I know with your talent you will help many children. I always tried to protect and help the children, and I hope I am somewhat responsible for your love for them.

Be happy, be safe, and know that you are loved,

Your father

It ended with the name and number of the guy she was supposed to contact, the promised bank names, account numbers, and figures. She was a millionaire, a multi-millionaire, and she hated her father for it. She'd wanted him in her life, and he gave her money she didn't care about and used her to clear his and Bello's names. He'd lied to her throughout her life; he was a manipulator and user. Of course this bland, bullcrap letter could just be more lies trying to make her feel like they'd had a relationship. It didn't change anything. Deathbed repentance wasn't something she had much sympathy for.

Zack rubbed her shoulder gently. She glanced up at him. Here was a real man. Someone who would cheer on his child, whatever they chose to do. Someone who would be patient enough to sit through dental appointments and lines at Disneyland, even if he hated every minute of it.

The air whooshed out of her. She had no right to be thinking about having children with Zack. She blinked and grasped for something else to focus on. "He really did trust Bello. Apparently they were working together to bring down other pirates?"

Zack studied her for a few seconds. She shook her head slightly; she couldn't deal with her dad issues right now. His lips pursed. He looked from her to Brooks. "Up until Bello turned on him."

Maddie nodded. "Bello must've been playing him pretty well." Bello was the son her father had always wanted, and look how that turned out. Karma.

She pushed her personal letter to the side—better to deal with those feelings later—and glanced over the papers for Homeland Security. The cover letter explained who her father was and what they had done to steal from many different boats throughout the past year. It said nothing of the crimes he'd committed before then. He asked them to help protect his wife and daughter until the rest of the pirate ring was captured. It included pages of maps that showed where the pirates liked to dock, hide out, and attack; there were specifications for the yachts they owned, but also a warning that they would infiltrate and take over any yacht they liked, so to watch closely for yachts that might be missing. It went on with where the pirates banked and went to regroup and which governments and individuals were giving them aid.

Maddie perused it all with Zack and Brooks watching over her shoulder, blinking back tears and praying they wouldn't notice. Anger welled in her chest. Her father thought giving her money would clear his name in her eyes. What a scuzz bucket. She didn't know what she'd hoped the letter would contain—something, anything to make her feel like he loved her and he wasn't a complete deadbeat father. Why couldn't he have been an undercover agent for the good guys?

Occasionally, one of the men would take a paper she'd finished with and read it more carefully. They all read their fill, and then Brooks and Zack sat in chairs on each side of her.

Brooks exhaled. "It appears your father was trying to right his wrongs by turning in all his former associates."

"Whatever helps him sleep in hell," Maddie choked out.

Zack took her hand. His warm fingers were a lifeline. She felt cold and lifeless. Her father had put her in danger so he could give her a bundle of money and make her responsible to bring other pirates to justice. The first trip he hadn't taken her mother on, and now she knew the reason. Why couldn't he have been man enough to turn himself in and give the authorities the information himself? He'd told her he was dying, but maybe he still had enough life in him that he didn't want to exchange it for prison. Yet, he'd thought this information would clear his and Bello's names.

She sighed, knowing her father too well. He'd rather be stabbed to death than spend even one night in jail. He hated to be cooped up worse than a skittish foal. It was like Bello had his knife in her gut as she realized that her father had, even in his last act, not done what would've been in her best interest. Weren't parents supposed to protect their children at all cost? She felt a sudden longing for her mom, but even she had a lot of explaining to do. Did her mom know why Maddie's father had brought her to his ship? That thought made her sick. No. Her mom would never allow Maddie to be in danger like this.

"Well." Brooks shoved his chair back and stood. "We can discuss and study all of this on the boat. I'd feel better if we started moving north."

Zack nodded. "Let me get a quick shower and grab some clothes." He squeezed her hand and then stood.

Maddie watched the men go. She carefully repacked everything into the packet, then stared out at the peaceful ocean. Her stomach was sour. The disappointment and ache for a father who cared made her wrap her arms around herself.

Was Bello even now headed their way? Bello must have changed his mind about turning in the other pirates and wanted the money and lifestyle instead. He must've known what the flash drive and packet contained to be so focused on getting them ... or did he want Maddie for his own sadistic reasons or some sort of twisted revenge against her father? She shivered despite the hot sun and warm breeze.

Brooks returned first, and his eyes were actually serious as he offered her a hand up. "We're going to take care of you, Maddie."

"Thank you." She didn't feel the attraction and connection to Brooks that she felt with Zack, but here was another man who was a natural protector and just an all-around good guy. Apparently they did exist, just not in her family tree.

"Sure. And when you get tired of runner man, you can always turn to me." His grin reappeared.

Maddie shook her head and laughed. "Glad to know the offer is always on the table."

CHAPTER EIGHT

Zack watched his island disappear behind them. He loved being there, but the adrenaline, attraction, and connection he was experiencing with Maddie made him realize he was getting bored with his lifestyle. He was comfortable being alone, but he really liked interacting with people, especially breathtaking brunettes.

Maddie laughed at something Brooks said, then shared a look with Zack. He couldn't believe she wasn't taken in by Brooks' charm like every other woman. Zack didn't blame the women, but Maddie was a breath of fresh air to him. All women seemed to think Brooks was handsome, with his flowing dark hair and megawatt smile, not to mention filthy rich and funny. Zack couldn't ask for a better friend, but he had no intention of giving Maddie up to him. Brooks could find hundreds of other women, and he probably would go through more than that before he settled down, if he ever settled down.

Maddie was the one for Zack. Sure, she was beautiful, but she was also well educated, funny, and cared about children. She hadn't freaked out or thrown a fit this entire trip, no matter how uncomfortable or scared she'd been. The disappointment of her father's letter showed on her face as she blinked to keep back tears, but instead of breaking down and bawling, she'd pressed on. Zack was impressed.

Settling back onto his cushion, he thought about making her his. They came from different worlds, and he didn't know how a relationship between them could develop. They lived on different continents and wouldn't see each other after they dropped her off at Key West tomorrow morning. Should he offer to stay with her? Would she want him to? He'd never had doubts if a woman wanted him before, but being alone the past two years had dulled his flirting skills and his confidence.

He glanced out the open rear of the boat, concentrating on the wake rolling behind them so he wouldn't stare at her nonstop. A white boat was coming from the south. Zack squinted. No. It couldn't be.

Could they outrun that yacht in Brooks' boat? His friend's yacht was fast, especially with the modifications he'd done, but not as fast as Zack's. He jumped to his feet and found the cupboard where Brooks kept his binoculars. His heart thudded heavily in his chest. It couldn't be the pirates. They should be coming from the north.

If it was them, how would he protect Maddie? She placed a soft hand on his arm. Zack jerked to look at her.

"What's going on?" she asked.

Brooks had turned around in his seat and was looking at him, quiet for the first time in forever.

"There's a white yacht coming up fast. I can't see the flags or determine if it's them yet."

Maddie swayed. Zack put an arm around her to hold her up. "It can't be ... can it?"

Zack's lips tightened. "I don't know. Maybe."

Brooks responded by pushing the throttle forward. The yacht accelerated in response. Would it be enough? "How fast can she go?" Zack asked.

"With the alterations I've done to her?" Brooks shrugged. "A little over forty-five knots."

Zack wasn't sure if that was a Sussurro, but they should be able to go the same speed as Brooks' Ferretti. He should've kept his boat instead of switching to Brooks' yacht to throw the pirates off their trail back on Cozumel. His boat could do close to fifty knots.

Brooks clung to the wheel, muttering quietly to himself. Zack held on to Maddie. "You doing okay?" he asked her.

She shook her head slightly. "I'm praying."

Zack smiled. "That's a great idea."

The smile and any thought of praying fled as he noticed the white yacht was closing in on them. He directed Maddie to a seat. "If they get closer, I'm going to have you go below."

She nodded, gave him a halfhearted smile, and bowed her head. Zack was amazed at her self-control; he'd never been much for whimpering or shrieking women. He liked that she was offering a prayer. It might be the only hope they had if that boat really was full of pirates.

He strode to Brooks' side. "How close are we to Cozumel?" he asked quietly.

Brooks glanced behind them. "Too far."

"You want me to take over?"

Brooks released his grip on the wheel. "I'll be back in a minute."

He disappeared down the stairs, returning a few minutes later with an arsenal. Maddie gasped, covering her mouth. "Is that really necessary?"

"Let's hope not," Brooks responded.

"Thank you," she whispered.

Brooks turned to her with arched eyebrows. "Thank me?"

"You're doing so much to watch out for me."

Brooks grinned. "Does that mean I'm getting a kiss after I protect you from these varmints?"

Zack's stomach tightened in protest. "I'd probably kiss you if you protect us."

Brooks scoffed. "No deal. I'm talking to Maddie."

Maddie gave an uneasy laugh. "How about a hug and a kiss on the cheek?"

Brooks hefted a machine gun and grinned. "I'll take it." His voice lowered. "And turn my head at the last instant."

Zack pushed at the throttle, but there was no give in it. They were at top speed, and the white yacht was still gaining. He kept an eye on the mirrors, not sure if it was the same boat, but it was hard to tell at this point. The flag was from Mexico instead of Italy like her father's boat, but they probably changed flags on a whim. They might have even changed boats. That would explain why they were gaining when Zack's boat had easily pulled away from them; he was going close to that speed now.

Brooks set up a machine gun and had a semi-automatic and several long-range hunting rifles on the back cushions.

"Can you look through the binoculars?" Zack asked Maddie. "See if it looks like your father's yacht. I don't think they could move this fast. Remember how we lost him in my boat? They shouldn't be catching us this quickly." He was trying to reassure himself as much as Maddie.

Maddie pressed the binoculars to her eyes for several long seconds. Finally, she pulled away. "I don't know. It looks like it, but I can't tell for sure without the flag to identify it."

Zack could see her hand trembling as she set the binoculars back down. The boat was still closing. "Steer for a second so I can look."

"Okay." She brushed past him and took the wheel. She looked so terrified with her eyebrows pinching together, lips thinned, and her entire body shaking. Zack wanted nothing more than to take her in his arms and reassure her it would all be okay, but this wasn't the time. He settled for a quick squeeze of her arm and a smile that he was sure she could read as fake.

"Should I start firing?" Brooks called back to them. "They're within range."

"No." Brooks sounded much too excited—probably hadn't had any combat opportunities for a while. "It might not be them."

"Killjoy," Brooks said.

Zack shook his head. Brooks was the best man he could imagine having around in a fight, but he loved to fight so much he often jumped in without thinking it through. Zack pressed the binoculars to his eyes and studied the lines of the boat for half a minute. It looked the same as her father's yacht, but there were other Sussurros in the Caribbean. "Were there other women with you on the yacht?" he asked Maddie.

She shook her head. "No."

"Unless they picked some up, this might not be Bello's boat." He studied it a little longer, clearly seeing several women sunbathing on the top deck. "I don't think it's them, though I'm pretty sure it's a Sussurro."

"Really?" Maddie let go of the wheel and grabbed the binoculars from him.

Zack took the controls, but warned her, "Let's keep watching them, but it looks like it's just somebody out to prove that their yacht is faster."

Maddie was nodding. "I don't recognize any of the people on that boat."

"Are you two saying I'm not going to get to shoot anybody?" Brooks sat back on his haunches and glared at them.

Zack laughed. "Not sure why that's making you grumpy."

"Well, I do like to use my guns, but I was also planning on getting a kiss out of the deal—and not from runner man." He winked at Maddie.

Zack ignored him, knowing he was just teasing. "I'm going to slow down a little bit and let them pass. If they try anything, I'm going to turn and make for home."

"Okay." Brooks settled back down behind his weapons. "Maybe if I'm lucky, they'll try something."

Zack slowed their speed, his hand poised on the wheel to make a quick turn if it did turn out to be the pirates. The boat approached, and several men came out onto the deck holding their drinks high and hollering at them. The women stood up and displayed a lot of skin as they cheered. Zack rolled his eyes, though relief poured through him. A bunch of drunk idiots, but not the pirates.

Brooks held up his gun and saluted all of them. One woman screamed and dropped her drink, while the others hooted and hollered like the machine gun was a prop at a party or something.

"What a bunch of imbeciles," Brooks said, grinning and waving.

"My thoughts exactly." Zack took one look at Maddie and gestured to his friend. "Come navigate for a bit."

Brooks took his weapons downstairs, then returned and took the wheel. Zack directed Maddie out front where they could have some privacy. The other boat was streaming away from them now. Brooks increased the speed to a comfortable rate again. Maddie shuddered as the boat sped up. Zack pulled her into his arms and sank onto a couch with her.

"You okay?" he whispered against her hair.

She nodded, but her trembling said otherwise. Laying her head on his shoulder, she let him hold her for a few minutes. The shaking subsided. She glanced up at him. "Am I ever going to be safe again? Am I ever going to *feel* safe again?"

Zack nodded, though he couldn't reassure her. He and Brooks couldn't stay and protect her once they were in America. He wanted to, but it wasn't his place. The authorities would take over. "Brooks could take on any ship of pirates with his arsenal. Before you know it, we'll be in the U.S. and you'll be done with us, and the authorities will protect you."

She stiffened in his arms. "I don't want to change my identity or be in protective custody," she muttered.

He didn't know how to reassure her about either thing. "It would be tough, but at least you'd be safe."

She pulled free of his embrace. "Thanks for watching out for me. I need to ... use the bathroom."

Zack watched her walk through the main cabin and down the stairs. He'd obviously not reassured her, but he wasn't the type to lie or offer empty promises. The worry gnawing at him, now that the other yacht was long gone, was all about if he would see Maddie again after this journey was through.

———

The rest of the morning was uneventful. Maddie talked with Brooks and Zack, but even Brooks was a little quieter, as if he could sense something was wrong. She was upset at Zack and trying her best to hide it. It was silly to be mad at him after all he'd done, but he didn't seem to have any desire to be with her after they made it to America, and was obviously planning to hand her over to the authorities and be on his way. He was more than willing to hold her, kiss her, and tell Brooks to back off, but he must see her as a quick fling.

Dang men anyway. Who needed them? Her hands unclenched. She was grateful for these two men's protection and going so completely out of their way to help her, but she wanted more from Zack. Much more. She needed to either get brave enough to see where he wanted to go from here, or give up dreaming about seeing him again once they reached America. It was just so hard when every other man she'd met paled in comparison.

She helped Brooks prepare sandwiches with raw veggies and cut-up fruit for lunch. Zack kept giving her these come-hither looks, but she didn't know how to talk to him without revealing how attached she'd become over the past two days. She wanted to help the authorities catch Bello and know she was safe from him, but she wanted to be with Zack more.

She concentrated on cutting apple slices so Brooks wouldn't see how upset she was. Zack had already done so much for her. She had no right to ask him to make a radical change and come spend time with her in Montana when he didn't even want to be in America. She sighed.

"What is all this *weepiness* about?" Brooks lowered his voice enough that Zack didn't even turn around at the question.

"Nothing." Maddie whipped up her head and forced a smile. "Thank you for taking care of me and feeding me."

"No. Uh-uh. This is not the Maddie that I've come to love and covet. Where's the spice? Tell me how I'm too full of myself or something." Brooks finished assembling a huge croissant sandwich, put some veggies and fruit on the plate, and said, "Wait a minute while I feed lover boy. You and I will take our lunch out back." He gestured with his head as if he knew she needed to get away from Zack and the underlying tension that kept growing between them.

"Okay," she whispered. She made a sandwich for herself and then grabbed water bottles out of the fridge.

Brooks' sandwich was already towering on his plate. He added some sides and pointed at the open patio. Maddie couldn't resist glancing at Zack as she walked out. He gave her a look of longing that made her want to forget about lunch and be with him some more, but that wasn't fair to him. She'd collided into his life and had no right to try to coerce him into staying with her longer than he wanted.

Setting her food on the back patio table, Maddie relaxed into the chair and took a second to soak the sunrays into her face. Ah. This was an amazing way to travel. Fresh air, sun, beautiful boat, handsome men. She glanced back at Zack one more time.

Brooks' booming laughter interrupted her perusal of the Most Beautiful Man in America. "You've got it bad, don't you?"

Maddie shoved a baby carrot in her mouth and muttered, "No, I don't."

Brooks had a mouthful of sandwich, so he luckily couldn't talk.

"Besides, I'll never see him again after we get to America, so what does it matter?"

Brooks swallowed and took a swig from his water bottle. "Ah. I see how it is. The poor girl is pining away for her man, and she hasn't even left him yet."

Maddie rolled her eyes and took a bite of her sandwich. It was very good, with fresh, savory meats and crunchy veggies on a buttery croissant.

"Why don't you just talk to him about it?"

The bite of sandwich stuck in her throat like a glob of bread dough. Maddie finally gulped it down and shook her head at Brooks. "Don't you dare say something to him."

Brooks reclined into the chair and grinned. "Why would you think I would meddle in your affairs?"

"I know your type."

Brooks chuckled. "No, you don't. You think I'm this super-good-looking buff rich guy who doesn't care about anyone but himself." He arched an eyebrow, challenging her to refute him.

"The selfish and rich part, yes." She couldn't quite hide her smile and started laughing.

"Yes! That's what I want to see. The laughing, happy Maddie who would tease me rather than kiss me." He winked, but then his face grew sober. "Truthfully, Maddie, I won't interfere, even though the biting of my tongue is killing me. It has to come from the two of you."

"Thank you." She nodded and took another bite of her sandwich.

"But I have to tell you that I've never seen my boy like this. Of course, the women usually come to me." He gestured to himself with a cocky grin. "But Zack has had his fair share of women hitting on him."

She remembered the conversation about that and how he'd acted like he didn't like it.

"I've never seen him this interested in or protective of any woman." He inclined his chin. "You've got something special with my boy. Don't screw it up by being a moody female."

"Moody female?" Maddie uncapped her water bottle and splashed it at him.

Brooks cried out in surprise and dodged away. He came out unscathed, but his sandwich got drenched. "Ah, no, you've ruined a masterpiece."

Jumping from his chair, he came at Maddie. She tried to stand and run from him, but he was too fast. He swooped her up and threw her over his shoulder. Hurrying down the steps to the ramp that was level with the water, he turned her upside down and dipped her hair in the salt water streaming past the boat. Maddie let out a combination of screaming and laughing that had Zack running to them. The boat swerved with no one steering it, and Brooks almost dropped her in the ocean.

Brooks backed away from the open sea and set her on her feet, laughing. Her wet hair trailed onto her dress. She smacked him. "This is the only dress I've got!"

Zack eyed the two of them. "Everything okay?"

"Yes." Brooks strode past him. "I think I'll go make myself another sandwich. Your chickadee ruined mine."

Zack studied her for a second. She couldn't quite wipe the smile off her face—partly because of Brooks' antics, but also because of what Brooks had said to her. Sometime today she was going to get brave and talk to Zack alone.

"You okay?" Zack asked.

"Yes." She squeezed the water out of her hair. "I'd better go shower."

He nodded, his eyes still much too serious. He turned and walked back up to the front of the boat. Maddie wished he would talk to her, but she straightened her back and promised herself she would be brave. Later. After her shower. Maybe tonight, when it was dark and she couldn't see his expression very well. She sighed and went through the lower entry to use one of the bathrooms.

CHAPTER NINE

Zack knew Brooks and Maddie's interactions were innocent and fun, but it bugged him all the same. Brooks was so much fun to be around, so charismatic, that women always fell for him. Zack clenched his teeth. He didn't want to feel like this about his best friend. But at the same time, this was the first woman he had staked a claim to; he was usually more than happy to let Brooks have all the attention and women. Brooks needed to respect that Maddie was his and back off. He grimaced. Maddie wasn't a possession, and she'd probably tell him off if she knew what he was thinking.

The afternoon dragged by with him in the captain's chair and Brooks and Maddie playing dumb card games. The lilting laughter he'd loved hearing from her now grated on his nerves. The sun dropped below the horizon, and Brooks strode toward him. "My turn to navigate, lover boy."

Zack nodded and backed away. "I'll throw together some dinner."

"That'd be great. Make Maddie help you. She's been a waste of skin on this trip." He tossed a wink Maddie's direction. She stuck out her tongue.

Zack headed to the kitchen without responding. Their flirtation was getting under his skin. Hopefully, after dinner Maddie would go sleep for a while, and by early morning they'd be in Key West. He'd never have to see her again and be tormented that she'd been interested in him until Brooks had turned on the charm. If his friend had any mercy in that huge body, Brooks wouldn't rub it in if he and Maddie kept in touch or developed a relationship. Not that a relationship with Brooks would last longer than a few weeks. They never did. At least that was some reassurance for Zack—that he wouldn't have to endure this jealous knot in his gut for a huge length of time.

He pulled out veggies and chicken to make a stir-fry. A different kind of worry lodged in his throat. What if Maddie was the one who finally broke through Brooks' wall of trust and was his friend's lifetime love? He swallowed hard. If that was the case, Zack would have to stop being selfish and conjure up some positive thoughts for his friend's happiness. He just didn't know why it had to be Maddie. The first woman Zack had really fallen for in ... he couldn't remember how long. He could spend years getting to know her funny personality and looking into her sparkling brown eyes, and it wouldn't be enough.

Maddie brushed up against him, and every nerve in Zack's body went into hyperdrive. He tried to control the burn in his stomach when his first instinct was to grab her and kiss her, even if Brooks was watching. Okay, maybe especially if Brooks was watching. Zack was too competitive; that was the problem. He'd never liked to lose, and that instinct to fight when he finally found the woman he wanted was over the top. It wasn't fair to his friend who had done more for Zack than any person but his mother and sister.

"What can I do to help?" Maddie glanced up at him with those liquid dark eyes.

Tell me you want me, then kiss me. Zack gulped down the words before they escaped. "Just watch the master chef work." He gave her a brave wink.

She grinned. "I can't wait to see the master chef in action again, but can I at least help chop veggies or something?"

"It's an art form. Shouldn't be messed with by amateurs."

Maddie's tinkling laughter had his chest swelling. He needed to think of a job for her quick, so she stayed with him rather than going to Brooks' side again. "But I could use a rice cooker. Very important job all on its own."

"I can do that. Where are the pots?"

He pointed down and watched unabashedly as she leaned over to grab a pot. Averting his eyes when she came back up, he caught Brooks laughing at him and shook his head at his friend.

"Rice?"

"They usually pack most of the dry goods in one of these upper cupboards."

"Got it." She found the rice and got to work measuring and mixing while he sautéed the marinated chicken with some diced onion and garlic.

"How would this be?" She shook her head at the well-stocked kitchen. "He just tells his people to stock it and they do."

Zack's shoulders tightened. She wanted this, what Brooks could provide. This wasn't Zack's mode of operation. He preferred taking care of himself, but he could make this happen for her too, if she was interested in him, not Brooks. "He has some great people who work for him. I could have the same if I wanted."

Maddie placed a warm hand on his arm. The chicken popped and sizzled in the pan, but Zack ignored it. "I'm sure you could; it's just not your style. I like that you take care of yourself."

"You do?" Zack inched closer to her.

"You're a very impressive man, Zack Tyndale."

Zack's hand moved of its own accord as he trailed his thumb down her soft cheek. "You're not so shabby yourself, Madeline Panetto."

She grinned and leaned into his hand. "Do you think that you and I—"

The stench of burning meat reached his nose at the same time as Brooks' holler. "What the—! Can't I trust you two to cook while I keep us safe?"

Zack turned back to the stove and salvaged the meat. He only had to cut off a small section of black, and luckily the open air of the cabin cleared out any burning smell. Maddie continued to help him by cutting up some fresh fruit and getting plates and utensils. The dinner turned out fine, but Zack really wished he'd been able to hear her finish her statement about the two of them.

Maddie helped clean up dinner with Zack, wishing she didn't notice his every movement. His athleticism was obvious in the way he moved, and she couldn't help herself from staring at times. They congregated by the captain's chair and chatted until it was late. Maddie was yawning despite their funny stories about living outside of America and the different customs and language barriers. Knowing these might be the last moments she had with Zack, she didn't want to go to bed.

"I'll radio the Coast Guard when we get a little closer, but we should be to Key West before you two beauties wake in the morning," Brooks said.

"You're staying up alone?" Zack arched an eyebrow. "That's mighty nice of you."

"I know you couldn't sleep through the night if you tried. Worrying about me and our little princess."

Maddie straightened. "I am not a princess."

Brooks winked. "Didn't mean to offend, love."

Zack scowled, but didn't say anything.

Brooks shooed them with his hand. "Go, rest. Come check on me when you wake up. You both look grumpy and exhausted. I need some peace and quiet, not irritable shipmates."

Zack arched an eyebrow at Maddie. "I don't think you look grumpy or exhausted."

"There he goes, twisting my words and trying to butter up the beautiful woman." Brooks winked at Maddie.

"Thank you for being the almighty Captain," Maddie said.

"No worries. It's a calm night and I need time to ponder and meditate."

Zack harrumphed. "He's never meditated a minute in his life."

"It's a new me," Brooks insisted, though his huge grin didn't back up his words. "Now go!"

Zack placed his hand on Maddie's back. The touch of his palm seared through the thin fabric of her dress. They walked through the main living area and down the stairs without saying anything. Zack guided her to a room. "There should be toiletries and anything you need in the shower."

"I know." She smiled. "I used it already when Brooks conditioned my hair with salt water."

Zack smiled, but it seemed forced. "You two had a lot of fun today."

Maddie tilted her head to the side and regarded him. Was he jealous? "We were just passing the time." She took a deep breath and forced herself to be brave. "I would much rather be with you."

Zack drew in a breath so quickly there was an audible pop. He blinked at her and took a step closer, his voice deep and husky. "You would?"

She nodded, not sure if she could trust her voice.

"But Brooks is so much fun to be with."

Maddie shook her head. "I'm not interested in your overconfident friend like that, Zack."

Zack's eyes darkened as he captured her gaze. He gently wrapped his hands around her upper arms. "Who are you interested in like that?"

Maddie swallowed, licked her lips, and then admitted, "You."

A slow smile grew on his handsome face. "I've been torturing myself all day."

"Stop."

He trailed his hands up past her shoulders and along her neck. Maddie shivered from the pleasant sensation and the smoldering look in his eyes. His fingers brushed her neck as he framed her face with his palms.

Maddie stared at him, unable to move or think.

"Not being close to you was killing me," he whispered.

He lowered his head, and their lips met in a soft caress. Zack groaned and increased the pressure and intensity of the kiss. Maddie grabbed on to his well-formed arms as he tilted her head with his hands and continued to kiss her with a passion she'd never experienced. His hands trailed around to her neck and down her back, leaving heat in their wake. Maddie clung to him and returned each kiss with her own.

"Slow your speed and prepare to be boarded." The words seemed to vibrate through the boat.

Maddie yanked back and opened her eyes. Bright lights flashed through the window. She froze. Bello? Moments later, footsteps pounded on the deck above them. Maddie held on to Zack as if he could protect her.

"It'll be okay," he reassured her.

Maddie knew the words were empty. Cold fear coursed through her body in an awful contrast to the warmth and joy of seconds before. Zack hurried her through the room and held his hand to the wall for a few seconds. A panel opened that she never would've noticed. "Hide in here. Don't come out for anyone but Brooks or me."

Maddie stood frozen in the constricted space.

"You'll be okay," he promised again before the door slid closed and cut him off from her.

She didn't dare move as she tried to control the panting sounds of her breathing. She could hear more footsteps and muffled voices above her. Was it really Bello? Had he somehow found them again? How could she just sit here? What if Bello killed Brooks and Zack to get to her? She could prevent that by giving herself up.

She said a quick prayer for strength and help, but didn't dare ask for protection. If it was Bello, and the Lord was merciful, she'd be dead before the night was over. Death was definitely preferable to being in Bello's clutches. She could protect Zack and Brooks if she made a deal with that devil.

Feeling around, she pushed against the secret compartment in several different spots before it finally slid open. The room was dark. She tripped and fell against the bed, quickly righting herself. She was almost to the door when it flung open. A man in dark clothing, holding an assault rifle, flashed a light in her face. "Identify yourself."

Maddie could hardly catch a breath for the fear choking her. "Madeline Panetto."

The man stepped back and gestured her out into the hallway. "After you, ma'am."

Several other men walked in and out of the lower rooms. One of them must've found Brooks' stash of guns, as he was toting quite a few of them.

Maddie walked through the hallway and climbed the stairs on rubber legs. Who were these men? They didn't seem like Bello's cronies, but she couldn't be sure. She ascended into the main cabin and caught Zack's eye. There was a small pile of weapons at his feet, and Brooks looked like he was taking a little harassment from one of the men. The man with the rest of Brooks' weapons came and set them next to the others.

"You like to be prepared, eh?"

"You try living in Mexico," Brooks threw back at him.

"It's illegal to own weapons in Mexico," the man said.

"You gonna arrest me?" Brooks smirked at him.

"They're U.S. Coast Guard," Zack said to Maddie.

"Are you serious? They showed you identification?"

"We had to show our identification and let him radio our superiors." One of the Coast Guard guys gestured to Brooks.

Zack nodded his confirmation of what he'd said. Maddie stumbled over one of the guns as she ran to him.

"Stop," someone commanded.

She ignored them and threw her arms around Zack. He held her close.

"The Coast Guard? We're saved!" Tears ran down her cheeks. She kissed Zack full on the mouth. He responded for a few seconds, then moved her to his side, keeping his arm around her.

"Madeline Panetto?" the man who had been talking to Brooks asked.

"Yes, sir." She wiped the wetness from her face with one hand. "Thank you for coming. How did you know?"

"Your mother received a message from your father early yesterday morning."

"Yesterday morning? He held them off all night?" Maddie knew a moment of gratitude for her father. He'd done everything he could to help her escape and find her help, even if it had been his fault she was in this situation to begin with. With the pressure of Zack's arm around her, it was hard to fault her father. She wouldn't have met Zack if all of this hadn't happened.

"I don't have all the details on that, ma'am, but we have captured his ship and the men who murdered him. They confessed to killing him."

Maddie did collapse then. Her father was dead, but she was safe. Zack held her up with his arm around her waist. "You caught them? You found Bello?"

"Not sure who Bello is, ma'am, but we've got the pirates in custody. I understand you have some papers for me that will help us find the rest of the pirate ring."

Maddie nodded to the drawer where they'd secured the papers. Brooks got them out and handed over the packet. "My father said to get them to Homeland Security."

"We're part of Homeland Security, so they're going to the right place."

Maddie smiled at him and turned to Zack. "They've captured Bello. I won't have to go into hiding!" She kissed him again.

There were a few whistles from the men; then a throat cleared, and she forced herself to turn back and face the guy in charge. Would he be the captain?

"Sorry, sir, this is just such a relief."

"I understand. You're going to have to come with us." He walked toward them and extended a hand.

Maddie clung to Zack, whose arms had tightened around her also. "But what about Zack and Brooks?"

"They're free to go with our gratitude for protecting you, but you are on our missing persons list and are also wanted for questioning. You'll need to come with us now." He took a hold of her arm; obviously now meant *right now*.

Maddie glanced up at Zack. She tried to memorize each line of his face. The warmth in his dark eyes. "It's been crack-a-lackin'. Thank you."

He grinned. "I thought it was better than crack-a-lackin'."

Warmth rushed into her face, and she wished she could kiss him again.

The Coast Guard dude tugged her from Zack's arms and directed her out the back patio and down to where a military boat was tied alongside the yacht.

Zack and Brooks followed them out. Maddie wanted to run back to Zack or shout out her cell number and demand he not forget it and come find her. Pathetically, she did nothing but wave and call to both of them, "Thank you." Then she was in the Coast Guard boat and the men loaded in behind her. Before she knew it, she couldn't even see the lights from Brooks' boat anymore. Tears flowed down her face. The guy in charge took her down to a sparse room.

"You're welcome to rest in here or come topside if you'd like. We'll be in Key West in about six hours, and then we'll fly you to D.C. Your mother is waiting there for you."

Maddie forced a smile. "Thank you." It was odd to thank someone for ripping her from Zack's arms.

He nodded and ducked back out of the door. Maddie sat on the bed, wrapped her arms around herself, and cried. It seemed hours ago that Zack was kissing her. Would she ever see him again?

CHAPTER TEN

"Well, hmm, this is awkward." Brooks stared Zack up and down. "Are you going to break down and bawl? Because I really am not good at the comforting stuff."

Zack blew air out of his nose in what he hoped was a convincing dissenting noise.

"Ah, man, you *are* going to cry." Brooks pounded him on the shoulder. "Let's just ... think of a game plan here. You know her name, that's something. What else we got?"

Zack could find her in Montana after she got through interrogation and went home, but he really wasn't doing this with Brooks. "Let's just go back to Cozumel. I want to get home."

Brooks shook his head. "That's a load of bull. No way am I falling for you being disinterested now."

"Brooks. Please just steer the boat. Maybe tomorrow I'll be ready for game plans, but I've got nothing right now." He stared at the spot where the Coast Guard cutter had disappeared. This boat was so empty without Maddie. Had she really been kissing him and telling him she was interested in him, not Brooks? It seemed like a faraway dream.

Brooks stared at him so plaintively he finally admitted, "I know where she lives. Let's go to Cozumel, and I'll drive my boat home, secure the island, and then fly to see her."

"You promise?"

Zack grunted a half laugh. "I don't know. Maybe. Okay?"

"You are the biggest wimp I know. If you don't promise, I'm just going to keep driving north until we hit the shores of the good old U.S. of A, and I'm going to force you to find her."

"She's going to need some time. Who knows how long she'll be with Homeland Security?"

"Okay. So give me a promise with a deadline."

Zack swallowed. "I promise to find Maddie in Montana within two weeks."

"Two weeks!" Brooks fired up the motor and started driving north just like he'd promised. "Nope. Here's our plan. We're docking in Key West, then we're flying to New York to see your niece for a few days, then we're going to Montana."

"You aren't doing this, Brooks.'"

"I am doing this. When my boy finally finds the perfect woman, I'm going to make it happen."

"All she said was thanks." Zack played over those last seconds as she was taken away. Why hadn't she asked him to come for her?

"What?" Brooks' voice was full of contempt.

"All she said was thanks when she left. She didn't ask me to come. She didn't give me any way to contact her."

"Stop being a wussy analyzer of the situation. Did you say anything substantial either? No! We were all in a state of shock after being boarded and having them harass me about having so many weapons. I didn't even say anything, and we both realize how unusual that is." He upped the speed. "We're doing my plan. You don't have to like it, but you're doing it."

Zack's body thrummed with desire to be with Maddie again. He was grateful Brooks had decided on a plan that would bring Zack to her. Having her taken away from him was torture, but the Coast Guard doing the taking at least reassured him she would be okay.

CHAPTER ELEVEN

Maddie made it through the boat ride and onto the flight to D.C. with only a few tears escaping. She was alone again, but at least she was safe. The pirates were captured, and her nightmare was over. Why couldn't she be happier? She closed her eyes and could picture Zack sitting on his dock with no shirt on, laughing up at her. Why couldn't she be with him right now? Would she ever see him again? All she knew was his name and that his island was north of Belize. It wasn't much to go on. She clutched the letter from her father. The Coast Guard had confiscated the forged passports and IDs, but they had left her the letter and told her she'd get the cash after the I.R.S. took out inheritance tax and cleared it. She had money now, lots of it. She could charter a boat and find Zack's island somehow, even if it took months.

She sighed and leaned her head against the seat on the plane. It would be worth it if she was certain Zack wanted her to find him. He'd definitely seemed to want her in his arms, but there just wasn't time to make a plan of reuniting or know his true intentions.

An hour later, she disembarked in D.C. and was taken to the Homeland Security office. The men had all been very kind to her, but she'd changed hands a few times and felt so displaced. No one and nothing were familiar.

Two men guided her into a sterile office. Maddie gasped when her mother spun to face her. Her dark hair was pulled back, and her large brown eyes were red-rimmed, but she still looked beautiful. She opened her arms, and Maddie flung herself into them. Her mom always smelled like the sweetness of gardenias.

"You're okay? They didn't hurt you?" Her mom leaned back and searched Maddie's face, running her hands over her arms. "Oh, my girl, I've been so worried!"

Maddie pulled away. She was relieved to be with her mom, but she had so many questions. "Why did you let me go with him? Why would you put me in danger like that?"

Her mouth dropped open. "I didn't know you'd be in danger."

"You didn't know your husband was a pirate?"

Her mom's mouth thinned. "You think I would've allowed you into that situation if I had known who he was associating with and what he would do?"

"Mom. You had to have known. All these years he's been lying to you. Didn't he have slimeball men with him?"

"No. We were always alone."

"But you had to sense something was off. Why didn't you just divorce him and cut off all ties?"

Her mom glanced at the two agents in the room who were watching their conversation with a little too much interest. She finally shrugged and admitted, "I loved him." A long pause, and then she sighed. "Our relationship worked for us. We only saw each other every few months, and it was new and exciting every time. He flew me to exotic locations, and it was like a honeymoon. I thought he was an international businessman like he always claimed."

"You had no questions?"

"He always answered them. Even took me to his office in Venice a couple of times." She glanced away from Maddie. "He was wonderful to me. My only regret was that he didn't spend more time with you."

"He always wanted you all to himself." Maddie grunted in disgust. "So you let a crooked man buy you off your entire life? I thought my mother was a tough, brilliant professor who raised me to be independent and strong."

Her mom flinched like Maddie had slapped her. "What do you mean, buy me off? He never gave me money."

"He didn't?" Did her mother really believe her own lame story?

"No." She shook her head quickly. "He bought me lots of gifts, and he paid to take me on extravagant vacations, but besides that, I provided for us and liked being my own woman. That's why our relationship worked so well. I would've been smothered by him being around all the time."

Maddie walked to a chair and sat heavily in it, trying to process all of this. She glanced up at her mother. "So, he called you two days ago?"

"He told me he was going to be killed by Bello soon and told me how to get the authorities alerted to find you and to capture the pirates. Made me write down so much information my fingers cramped." She pressed her lips together, and a tear leaked out of the corner of her eye. "And now he's gone."

Maddie stood and went to her mother. She hugged her. It was weird that Maddie had little remorse for her father dying when it was obviously ripping her mother apart. She couldn't even imagine wanting a marriage like the one her mother had described, but she'd witnessed it her entire life, and she did know that her mom had seemed happy with her lot in life. So odd.

The men gave her mom a few minutes to compose herself; then they started in on the questioning. It lasted for hours. They broke for snacks, drinks, and lunch, but besides that, they grilled Maddie and her mom on different interactions throughout their lives with her father and most specifically in relation to the pirates. When Maddie told the story of Zack and Brooks helping her, her mother eyed her suspiciously, but luckily didn't start her own line of mother questioning.

The next day they were informed that most of the pirate ring had been captured, and it was safe for them to go home. The flight home was full of too much soul-searching, as Maddie didn't know what she wanted to do with herself when she got there. She'd let her college apartment go when she graduated. She and her friend, Abby, had planned to buy a house together, so right now all of Maddie's stuff was in her mom's garage, and she was staying back in her old room in her mom's basement.

It was surreal to be home. Zack seemed years and planets away from her now. She knew if she told Abby the story, her friend would put off looking for jobs with her newly acquired MBA and go search for him, but Maddie still wasn't sure if that was the best course. She wasn't starting her new job until August, a few weeks before the new school year started. This was supposed to be a summer to relax, play, and find a house. Now she wasn't sure what to do with herself, except pray that she could forget about Zack or get brave enough to chase after him.

CHAPTER TWELVE

Zack paid the cab driver, and he and Brooks climbed out of the back. Neither of them had much more than a small bag. Brooks whistled as he looked around at the imposing gate and guardhouse. The main house peeked from behind the rows of trees and a fence. "I've never been to the family manor. A little stuffy, but I kinda like it."

Zack didn't respond. He liked everything about the massive brick home where he'd grown up in Greenwich, Connecticut. The town had a lot of open space, and he'd had plenty of freedom as a boy to explore and run. The house was after the Colonial style, and because his father was usually away on business or working long hours in the city, the house had mostly good memories for him.

He and Brooks hadn't called to say they were coming, so he wasn't even sure if his mom or niece would be here. He walked over to talk to the guard. It was much easier than trying to get a taxi into the fortress. A limo pulled up next to him. The back door popped open and his niece leapt out. The guard wasn't familiar to Zack, and he immediately moved to intercept Chalise.

"It's okay, Sam." His mother climbed out of the backseat and hurried to his side.

Zack swooped Chalise into his arms and savored the smell of baby lotion and sweetness. She grinned broadly at him, kissing his cheek before settling against his chest. Zack swallowed against his emotions as his mom descended on them.

"Zack, sweetheart," his mom gushed. "You're home!"

Zack shifted Chalise to his right arm and hugged his mom close with his left. They simply held each other. Zack could've stayed like this all day, but his mom backed away and wiped at her eyes. "I can't believe you're here. How long are you staying?" She glanced around for luggage and spotted Brooks. "Oh." Her eyebrows arched up. "You brought a ... friend?"

Brooks cackled. "Not that kind of friend."

His mom blushed.

Zack gestured. "This is my buddy, Brooks. I've told you about him."

Brooks came forward and gave his mom a hug. "Nice to meet you, Momma."

She gave a very uncharacteristic giggle. "Oh! You as well, Brooks."

Zack grinned. Leave it to Brooks to charm his fifty-year-old mother. He glanced over at her. She was still fit and dressed perfectly in a red silk shirt and black-and-white-striped pencil skirt. Her blond hair and beautiful face hadn't changed in years. He wondered if she'd had plastic surgery, but would never ask.

"Let's go inside." She gestured the car on, and the four of them walked up the driveway lined with oak trees.

Chalise was still cuddled into Zack. She darted a glance up at Brooks, then tucked her head back in. It was a warm June day and sweat popped up on Zack's forehead.

"And who is this pretty girl?" Brooks asked, tilting his head down to meet Chalise's gaze.

Chalise smiled shyly at him, but of course didn't answer.

"Chalise." His mother's voice took on the soft tones reserved for her granddaughter. "Can you say hello to Uncle Zack's friend?"

Chalise pushed her lips out in a stubborn expression that almost made Zack laugh, but she lifted a hand in greeting. Brooks took the fingers in his and kissed them as they walked slowly. Chalise grinned broader, but didn't giggle like most little girls would have.

"It's nice to meet you, Princess Chalise."

Everyone held their breath, hoping she would respond, but nothing happened besides a slight red tinge to her light brown skin. Zack didn't want anyone to pressure her. He loved Chalise no matter what, but he couldn't help wondering if she would ever talk.

"So how long are you staying with us?" his mom asked.

"A couple of days," Zack answered.

"Oh, darling. You finally come home and you're only staying a couple of days." His mom's mouth pursed, but no wrinkle lines showed.

"Sorry, Mom. This was all kind of ..." He glanced at Brooks, who was smirking at him. "Last-minute."

"What's going on?"

They walked up the concrete steps to the wide front porch. Brooks held the door for everyone, and his mom directed them into the front sitting room. "Are you hungry?" she asked before Zack could answer her last question.

"No." Zack looked at Brooks.

"I'm fine."

A uniformed maid came into the room. Her gaze darted between Brooks and Zack. "Can I get you anything, ma'am?"

"Some water and lemonade. Thank you, Ally."

"My pleasure." Her eyes lingered on Brooks before she swept out of the room.

Zack sat with Chalise on his lap. His mom sat next to him, with Brooks filling up a dainty chair.

"Tell Uncle Zack about your dance lessons," his mom urged.

There was a pause as his mom leaned forward and gave Chalise an encouraging smile. Zack would love to hear her answer, but he didn't think the constant pressure and hope was helping. Chalise bobbed her head to the side and smiled, but didn't say anything.

The silence was too much to bear, and Zack was relieved when Brooks turned to his mom. "Zack's met the love of his life, and we're going to chase her down."

The relief fled as Zack's neck heated up. "Brooks! Seriously?"

"You'd tell her anyway. I know you tell your momma everything."

His mom's eyes were soft as she squeezed Zack's arm. "Truly? You've met someone?"

"Yes." He fought the grin, but couldn't hide it from his mom. "But I don't know if she wants to be with me."

"Any woman would want to be with you," his mom insisted.

The maid brought in a tray with a carafe of water and various kinds of individual lemonade flavors.

"True," Brooks said. "Unless I'm around." He winked at the maid, who blushed and almost dropped the tray.

His mom waited until they all had a drink and the maid was gone before leaning into Zack. "Why would you say something like that? Of course she'd want to be with you."

"Don't listen to him," Brooks insisted, sipping his strawberry lemonade. "She told me she wants him. He just needs to grow some, ahem, guts."

His mom blinked at Brooks, obviously not accustomed to his manner of speech.

Zack pulled out his phone and opened the photos. There were dozens of pictures of his island and Belize. He knew Chalise would love all the pictures of the local children who liked to sell him stuff when he went for supplies. He handed it to the little girl, who grinned up at him and started scrolling through.

"It's a really long story, Mom, but I promised Brooks that in two days I would go to Montana and try to find Maddie."

"Maddie? Montana?"

Zack loved his mother, and he'd always shared a lot with her, but he was exhausted from traveling, worrying about Maddie, and the tension of being back in America. Despite his hat and sunglasses, a pair of college-aged girls had recognized him at the airport. They asked to take a selfie with him and then wanted him to sign their arms with a marker. Thankfully, Brooks had joked with them and the men had been able to escape.

"Brooks?" Zack looked to his friend. "You on?"

Brooks grinned. "Because I am the master storyteller, my boy has just given me permission to share his." He clucked his tongue. "Fill in any holes, my friend."

Brooks proceeded to share Maddie's story with his mother. Zack held his niece and answered questions or clarified points along the way. He realized it was insane to want to be with someone after knowing her for two days, but his mom didn't give any indication that's what she thought. She kept glancing at Zack with warm smiles. Zack was glad to be with her and Chalise again, but he knew the next two days were going to drag until he could get to Maddie.

CHAPTER THIRTEEN

Maddie walked in the house late. She dropped her stuff off in her room and went back upstairs to raid the fridge and try to find something palatable. She missed Zack's cooking. Sighing, she flipped the hair off her neck. It was hot in the house. She missed Zack more than his yummy food.

She and Abby had spent the entire day touring houses. She hadn't told her friend that she'd be able to pay cash for her half of the mortgage. It was still pretty foreign to think of all that money, and she wasn't sure if she wanted to use it. The government had cleared it, so it must be clean, but she didn't like the thought of her father buying her off on his deathbed. It would be fun to use the money to buy the house for her and Abby, but she knew Abby too well and knew something like that would tick her off.

Her phone rang.

"Hey, Abby."

"I'm just dying over that great house on Quinn Creek. I loved all the rustic details mixed with the modern updates, and the windows and view are amazing!"

"It would be a nice, quiet spot. I swear, though, are we twenty or eighty? We should probably be looking at condos close to the university." She pulled out a cheese stick and an apple. It was a lame dinner, but it would work.

"Pshaw. We've done that scene. I want tranquility. I want to plant a garden."

"What am I going to do living out there all alone when Russ proposes next month?"

Abby chortled. "You wish."

"I wish! I thought you wished." Maddie peeled off some of the cheese and popped it in her mouth.

"I don't know if it's right, Maddie-girl. I mean, we've been dating for a year, and if I haven't had that confirmation yet, what does that say?"

Maddie choked on the cheese. She'd known Zack two days and ached for him every minute since they'd been pulled apart by the Coast Guard. What did that mean? Was that the confirmation Abby was talking about? But falling hard and fast wasn't a smart way to start a relationship.

"Hello? Are you there?"

Maddie swallowed. "You just don't feel right about it, do you?"

"Nope. But that's okay. There are a lot of hotties just waiting to meet me."

Maddie laughed. "For sure."

"Like Zack Tyndale." Abby said his name on a dreamy sigh. "You actually met him, and it sounds like he was into you. Someday I'll find mine."

Maddie nodded, though her friend couldn't see her. She'd googled Zack and his pictures more times than she wanted to admit over the past couple of days. She'd studied, or rather drooled over, the images. Brooks had told her Zack was a changed man, and he did seem different now that she knew him. There was a sparkle in Zack's eyes that was absent in those pictures. She liked to think the sparkle was reserved for her.

"I want to go find him," she admitted to Abby.

"Really?"

Maddie heard a tapping like footsteps. She whirled around to look, but saw no one. Must've been something outside. Her mom was meeting with their pastor again tonight. On Sunday, they were going to hold a funeral service of sorts for her father. She hoped it would give her mom some closure.

"Let's do something crazy." Maddie set the cheese on the counter, her stomach churning too much to eat right now. She pulled in a quick breath, then spit out the words. "Before we settle down to work and be old maids, let's fly to the Caribbean, charter a boat, and go find Zack."

Abby let out a whoop. "You know I'm in, baby! But ..." The excitement in her voice faded. "That might take our whole down payment for this house."

"My dad left me some money. I'll pay for the trip."

"What? Why didn't you tell me? Let's do this!"

Maddie grinned, but the smile left her face as she felt the cold pressure of steel against her neck. She flipped her hand back to push away whatever it was. Time seemed to stop as her hand made contact with what could only be a pistol. She jerked forward away from the weapon, and then spun to face it. A scream ripped from her throat.

"What?" Abby yelled in her ear.

The air whooshed out of her lungs. Her legs trembled, and she almost dropped the phone. Pointing a handgun at her was Bello. His dark eyes flickered over her body, then back to her face. He was not smiling. He gestured to the phone with his gun. "Say goodbye and act natural."

"Nothing. It's nothing." Maddie was panting and couldn't help it. "I saw a spider. I gotta go. Let's chat tomorrow."

"Okay. Love ya."

"You too." Maddie ended the call, clinging to her phone and staring at Bello. It was hard to think clearly with him standing in her house and that gun in his hand.

"Drop the phone," he commanded.

She let it go. It clanged against the wood floor. "What are you doing here?" she finally managed to get out.

"I came for my money and a chance to have a little fun with you." He smirked at her. "Before I kill you, like I did your father."

A rush of hot injustice simmered in Maddie's stomach. It was an odd contrast to the cold sweat trickling down her back. "He trusted you."

Bello shrugged. "His mistake. I acted as if I wanted my name cleared with the authorities like he'd always dreamed of, but it was always about the money. In case he tried to turn the information in without me knowing it, I put a tracking device on the flash drive. He fought all night long, that should make you proud. If he'd given up sooner, we would've captured you that night and saved both of us a lot of time. Where are the papers he gave you?"

"I don't have them." Maddie tilted her chin up. "I gave them to Homeland Security."

Bello smacked her in the side of the head with the gun. Maddie crashed to the wood floor. Warm blood trickled down through her hair. She saw black for a few seconds before her vision cleared and a strumming pain raced through her head.

"Get up," he snarled.

Maddie held on to a side table and forced her legs underneath her. It took a few seconds to drag herself to her feet.

Bello watched her with a sneer. He grabbed her elbow and yanked her against his body, placing the gun to her temple. "Your dad coded the accounts. Homeland Security cleaned out all of my accounts before I could access them, but I know your father had separate accounts for you. He squealed everything when we started cutting him."

Maddie's stomach dropped and her throat went dry. She wanted to scratch his eyes out. He was pure evil.

"Do you want to end it all right now, Maddie, or do you want to give me the bank account numbers?"

Maddie's heart thumped uncontrollably and it made her injured head hurt worse. She didn't care about the money, but she knew Bello would rape and kill her as soon as he had it. If only she could've given Abby some signal on the phone.

"The p-paper is in my room." Her body trembled. She had to think of a way to escape.

"Well, isn't that perfect?" He smiled, white teeth flashing against his caramel skin. "We'll be near a bed, so I can take care of you after I transfer my money."

Maddie's stomach churned and acid crawled up her throat. She prayed she would throw up all over Bello. Maybe that would at least keep him from forcing himself on her. He yanked her down the hallway. "Which room is it?"

Maddie prayed and prayed. The thought of being downstairs alone with him wasn't a good one. If she kept him on the main floor and directed him to her mom's room, at least there was a chance she could escape through her mom's French doors and run for the neighbors.

"Down this hall," she managed to get out through a throat thick with fear. "How did you escape?" she muttered.

"Escape?" Bello eyed her strangely.

"The Coast Guard said they caught you."

He chuckled. "No, they never caught me. They caught your dad's crew. I secured a new boat shortly after you escaped from me in Cozumel and sent the rest of them toward Key West, knowing if you had the papers the Coast Guard would be looking for us."

Maddie had to hand it to him. He was smart. They entered her mother's master suite. Maddie walked stiffly toward the desk that rested against the exterior wall. If she could distract him and make it to that door, she might have a chance of living through the night.

She made a show of opening a drawer and shuffling through the papers. On top of the dresser, an award her mother had received from the university caught her eye. She closed the drawer. "I thought I put it in there, but it's under this plaque."

"Just get it," Bello muttered impatiently.

Maddie wrapped her hand around the heavy glass award. She lifted it up and took the top paper that was underneath it. Extending the paper to Bello, she released it before he wrapped his fingers around it. He cursed and leaned forward slightly to pick it up. Maddie jabbed the heavy glass object as hard and fast as she could forward, making contact with his forehead. His head swung backward and he fell against the bedpost.

Maddie sprinted for the outside door. A gunshot rang out, slamming into the wall, less than a foot from her head. Maddie screamed, ducking and ripping the door open. She didn't want to give Bello a chance to get up off the floor or improve his aim.

She flung herself out the door, falling down the concrete steps. Thankfully, she caught herself against the railing and made it to the patio. How she wished for her phone! She ran all out toward the Kings' back patio. Warm yellow light spilled out of their back windows. They were home. If she could just make it there—

Loud steps pounded down the stairs behind her, and Bello's gun discharged. The bullet burrowed into a tree next to Maddie, sending sprays of bark against her face. She screamed and covered her face.

"Stop!" Bello commanded. "That was a warning. The next shot will be in the back of your head."

Maddie had no desire to obey his command. The thought of a bullet in her head made her want to vomit. Her running speed decreased as her legs weakened with fear. She begged a merciful Father in Heaven to protect her. *Please let me make it to the Kings'*. She was so close. Flying up their wooden deck stairs, she wondered why Bello hadn't shot again. Did he want her alive?

Maddie rushed across the deck and flung open the patio door. Mr. and Mrs. King were watching television, each seated in an easy chair. "Call the police!" she screamed, slamming the door shut behind her and turning the deadbolt.

Mr. King reached for the cordless phone on the side table. "You okay, Maddie-girl?"

"No! A man is trying to kill me."

He sat straighter. "I thought I heard a gunshot and a scream, but wasn't sure with the TV show so loud." He gestured to his frail wife. She'd always had trouble hearing, and being over eighty hadn't improved her condition.

"Please, call 911." Maddie had no clue where Bello was or what he would do when he caught up with her.

He nodded and started dialing the number. Mrs. King's mouth fell open. She pointed behind Maddie. Maddie whirled and had to cling to the door handle so she wouldn't fall to the floor. Bello stood next to the open window, his gun pointed at Mrs. King through the screen and a horrible mocking smile on his face.

"You come with me now, Maddie, and I won't kill your friends."

Maddie glanced back at Mrs. King. Her face was pasty white, and she was shriveled under her mint-green afghan as if it could protect her from the bullet.

"Drop the phone," Bello told Mr. King.

The older man obliged, dropping the phone into his lap and lifting his hands up. Mrs. King's lip quivered and she closed her eyes and ducked her head. Maddie had no choice. She couldn't allow these kind neighbors and lifelong friends to be hurt if she could help it. Unlocking the deadbolt, she opened the door a fraction and slipped outside, closing it quickly behind her. She strode past Bello.

"Let's go," she said in what she hoped was a confident voice.

Bello shook his head. "Did you think it would be that easy?"

"Please don't kill them." Maddie panted for air, looking back through the window at the older couple, who both looked inches from death because of the paleness of their faces and their wide-eyed expressions.

Bello swung the door open, pointing his pistol at Mrs. King again. "Toss me the phone, old man."

Mr. King threw it at him. It skidded past them onto the deck. Bello bent to pick it up. Maddie rammed her shoulder into the side of his abdomen. Being already bent over, he toppled onto the deck. She hated to run with the Kings right there and in danger, but she had to believe Bello would follow her.

Pounding down the patio stairs, she raced around to the front of the house. She honestly had no clue where she was going except for away from Bello. He screamed from behind her and within seconds she could hear his footsteps racing after her. Maddie kept running, pebbles and twigs jabbing into her bare feet.

Headlights approached from the street in front of her house. Maddie ran for them. She dodged in front of the car, leaping at the last second. The car barely missed her. Brakes and tires squealed. A loud thump came from the front of the car and Maddie was instantly reminded of the time she'd hit a deer back in high school. She whirled around to see Bello fly off of the bumper and crumple to the ground.

Maddie ran around to the driver's side. The door popped open and her mom climbed out. "Maddie! What on earth?"

"Call 911. Bello. Here!" She pointed at the body on the ground.

"Oh my!" Her mom's hand flew to her mouth. She reached back into the car and dug her phone out of her purse.

Maddie shifted nervously from foot to foot as her mom told the dispatcher what had happened and begged them to hurry. She studied Bello's body, terrified he was going to pop up and come after her any second. She should probably go check if he was still alive, but she couldn't force herself to do it.

Mr. King toddled out onto his front porch, brandishing his cordless phone. "The police are coming," he shouted bravely.

"Oh, thank you," Maddie hollered back. "Mom hit him with her car."

"Good job, Vanessa."

Her mom's eyebrows arched up. "How does Mr. King know what's going on?"

"It's a long story." Maddie glanced back to check on Bello. A scream ripped from her throat. His body was gone. "No, no, no!" She pushed her mom. "Get in the car. Get back in your house!" she yelled to Mr. King.

He complied, shutting the door behind him. Her mom was another story. She fought against Maddie, shoving Maddie into the car first. Maddie fell against the gearshift, grunting in pain. "Mom, no!"

Bello hobbled up behind her mom and pushed his gun into her head. "And this is Armando's wife. The lovely Vanessa I've heard so much about. How charming."

Her mom slowly turned to face him. Maddie slid out of the car and stood next to her mom. "Leave her out of this. I'll get your paper. You can have me."

Bello nodded. "Let's all go for a walk. Your beautiful daughter has a paper I need. Then I need to enjoy her body before I kill you both." Bello growled out the last sentence. He limped behind them, dragging his right leg, as they walked stiffly toward the house. Maddie took some satisfaction that he was hurt. Maybe he wouldn't be strong enough to do what he wanted.

Her mom squeezed her hand. Maddie's stomach dropped. "No, Mom," she whispered. Her mom had taken some self-defense classes at the university and had confided in Maddie how excited she was to try them out. Now was definitely not the time. Bello was a trained killer.

"Stop talking!" Bello yelled.

Her mom whirled and kicked his arm. The gun went off. Maddie screamed, not sure if the bullet had hit her mom or not. Bello cursed loudly as her mom slammed her fist into his nose.

Maddie grabbed Bello's hand that still held the gun with both of her hands and tried to rip it from him. His grip was too strong. He raised the gun slowly, with Maddie fighting with everything she had to take the weapon away.

Her mom chopped at his arm with both of her hands like she was a karate ninja or something. Bello howled and released his grip enough for Maddie to strip the gun from his fingers. Bello whirled on her mom and started pounding her with his fists. Maddie pointed the gun at Bello.

"Stop! I'll shoot!"

"You will not," he sneered.

"She might not, but I will." A loud voice came from behind Bello.

He whirled around. Maddie looked past him to see two policemen with weapons drawn. She released all her air and followed their instructions to set the gun down and back away. The officers wasted no time cuffing Bello and dragging him away. Maddie turned to her mom.

She was shaking and disheveled.

"Are you okay?" Maddie asked.

"Yes." She flexed and extended her fingers, then messed with her jaw a little bit. "I told you those classes would work."

"Oh, Mom." Maddie hugged her.

"It's okay," her mom whispered into her hair. "I couldn't let him hurt you."

Maddie squeezed her tighter. "I love you." She realized her mom would never have sent her into danger with her father. She had to fight back tears.

"I love you, sweetheart."

Mr. King toddled down his steps and over to them. His chest was puffed out. "I told the police everything that was going on and how they needed to come in real sneaky-like. They parked over at the Jensens' and snuck right through all those trees."

"Thank you," Maddie gushed, hugging him and kissing his rough cheek.

"I'm baking you a pumpkin pie tomorrow," her mom promised.

"Well now." Mr. King grinned. "A kiss from a beautiful lady and a pie from another. That was worth any danger I put myself in."

"Harold!" Mrs. King called from the porch. "Stop flirting with the girls."

Mr. King grumbled good-naturedly as he went back to his wife's side. The policemen separated them and asked Maddie and her mom questions. Maddie couldn't believe it was really over. Bello was arrested and she was finally safe. Tomorrow she was going to start researching and find a guide to help her find Zack.

CHAPTER FOURTEEN

Zack and Brooks waited on the front porch as the family limousine pulled around from the garage. They'd chartered a plane to go to Montana. The last two days had been a great time to reconnect with his mom and niece, and he'd only had one confrontation with his father. Brooks was able to diffuse the situation pretty quickly, and it didn't hurt that his father had instantly connected with his loud friend. It had been nice to be home after two years, but he was chafing to find Maddie. He didn't know what he would say to her or how they were going to start a relationship, but he had to give it a try.

His mom gushed over him and hugged him multiple times. "Please come visit us again," she begged.

"If you promise to bring Chalise down for a couple of weeks, then I'll come here after that."

"Deal." She stuck out her hand, and they shook on it. Zack smiled. He sure loved his mom.

He squatted down next to Chalise, and she threw her thin arms around him. "Love you, sweetie," he said. "Grandma will bring you to see me soon."

He pulled back and searched her eyes, praying she knew how much he loved her.

"Tell Uncle Zack you love him," his mother prompted.

"Mom," Zack warned quietly. "She's okay. She'll say it when she's ready." He straightened and lifted Chalise into his arms, never wanting to let her go.

Chalise burrowed into his neck and hugged him tightly. "Don't leave, Uncle Zack," she whispered in his ear.

Zack jerked in surprise. It took everything in him to control his response and not just dissolve into a puddle of tears. She'd spoken to him. He swallowed and finally managed to say, "I don't want to leave you. Shall we see if we can talk Grandma and Grandpa into letting you go with me?"

"Yes, please," she whispered.

Zack glanced at his mom. Her mouth was open and tears streamed down her cheek. "Did she just say 'Yes, please'?"

"She whispered 'Don't leave, Zack' first," he managed to get out. He was so thrilled to hear her speak but didn't want to make too big of a deal out of it. He loved her no matter what.

Brooks grinned and nodded. "Nice, Chalise."

"She needs to be with me, Mom," Zack said.

His mom shook her head, but didn't say anything.

"Let me take her with me to Montana, and then back to the island for a little while. She needs me. Has she spoken to anyone else?"

"You know she hasn't," his mom snapped. She folded her hands in front of her, squeezing her fingers together. "But I can't let her go. She's all I have."

"You can come with us too."

"Your father needs me here. This is my home."

Zack looked to Brooks for help. He lifted his hands. "Your family battle, man. I got nothing."

His father walked out onto the front porch. Zack had assumed he'd already gone to the office for the day. He shook Brooks' hand. "It was nice to meet you, young man. Come again."

"Thank you, sir, I will."

Sterling turned to his wife, and the smile left his face. "What's wrong?" He glanced at Zack clinging to Chalise. "What did you do?"

"He didn't do anything," his mom was quick to say. "Chalise spoke."

His father stuttered back a step. "She ..." He shook his head and pressed his knuckle against his teeth. "What did she say?"

Zack just stared. His dad really did love Chalise, but it was conditional like the love Zack had known his entire life. *If you work for me, I'll love you. If you speak, I'll love you.* Yet, Zack knew what he needed to do for himself and Chalise. It came to him so fast, he didn't even think as he spit out the words, "I'll work with you, Dad."

His dad grinned.

"If you'll let me have custody of Chalise."

His mother's lips tightened. Sterling put an arm around his wife's waist. She leaned heavily against him. Zack didn't want to cause them pain and rip their granddaughter from them, but he knew this was right.

He rushed on before his dad could start rebutting. "You'll get to see her anytime you want, but I think she needs to be with me. She told me not to leave, Dad."

Sterling's jaw worked, and he shook his head.

"I need her with me," Zack said.

"Here in New York." His father's words were never a question, but a demand.

Zack wouldn't commit to that. He loved his mom and could see his dad was trying with Chalise, but he and Chalise needed to be away from the pressure and demands. "No. I want to work from the island so I can be with Chalise rather than put her in day care."

His mother gave him a measuring look. She didn't put Chalise in day care, but Chalise spent far too many hours with therapists and the nanny.

That look crossed his dad's face like they were about to have a battle, but Zack held up a hand. "You know I can get everything done through my computer and phone. I'll fly in one week a month to work from the office and so you can both spend time with Chalise. When I travel for work, you can keep her ... and, of course, you're both welcome to come visit us anytime."

The silence was thick as everyone waited for his father's response. Seconds ticked by, and Zack didn't know if he should keep arguing or just pray.

Chalise lifted her head off Zack's shoulder. "Please let me live with Uncle Zack, Grandpa."

They all gasped. The words were so clear, so perfect. Zack brushed away the tears that formed at the corners of his eyes. He squeezed her tighter.

His father's jaw slackened. He smiled tenderly at Chalise. "If that's what you want."

Zack swallowed hard and blinked to hide the emotion that was racing through him. He got to keep Chalise. She was talking. He wanted to punch a fist in the air. He really wanted to tell Maddie.

Sterling stepped toward them and opened his arms wide. "But you're going to have to give me lots of hugs and kisses."

Chalise leaned toward him, and Zack let her leap into her grandpa's arms. Sterling held her close as she hugged him and kissed his cheek. Zack had never seen his dad like this. He had shut the man out of his life the past two years and was shocked at this soft side. It gave him hope that they could learn to work together in a better way than they had before. Even if they couldn't, it was worth hard days with his father to have Chalise with him.

Sterling smiled at Zack over the top of Chalise's head. "I need a week here, bringing you up to speed at the office first; then you can go to your island for a couple weeks."

"Three-to-one ratio," Zack reminded him, rubbing at his head. This was going to be tough. "And I need to make a little detour to Montana first."

"Montana?"

Brooks hooted. His mother shook her head and gave Zack a sly wink. Chalise stared at him. "What's Montana?"

Zack grinned. "We're going to see a lady that I think you will like very much."

His dad and mom exchanged a look. "Well," Sterling said, "if the boy is finally ready to settle down, maybe a trip to Montana is okay."

"Thanks." Zack didn't know if he could trust this new and improved version of his father, but he wouldn't complain. He was going to have custody of Chalise, and soon they'd both be with Maddie.

CHAPTER FIFTEEN

Maddie had done some research and found a couple different options for chartered yachts docked in Belize. She was most intrigued by an older gentleman named Captain Sam, who seemed very competent and had been sailing near Belize for almost twenty years. If anyone could find Zack's island, it would be him.

The thought of seeing Zack again had her insides quivering. Would he be excited to see her or think she was much too forward to come after him? At least she'd have Abby with her. That would help ease the awkwardness. If he didn't act thrilled to see her, she could claim they'd just chartered the boat to show Abby where she'd been and say hi. She laughed to herself. That was lame and she knew it.

The doorbell rang, and she closed her laptop. She needed to stop researching and go enjoy the beautiful summer night, anyway. Later tonight she'd put down her deposit with Captain Sam, and by next week she'd be in the Caribbean, possibly seeing Zack. It would be a dream come true, but she still loved her Montana home and wanted to spend as much time outside as possible before she left.

She flung open the front door, and her eyes dropped to a darling little girl with crazy black curls. She'd seen her before, but where?

"My Uncle Zack would like to request your presence at dinner tonight," the tiny cutie said quickly, then gasped for a breath.

Maddie's heart seemed to stop, then thundered in her chest. She searched the road but didn't see anyone. Bending down, she smiled at the little girl. "I would love to. Where is your Uncle Zack?" Just saying his name brought tremors to her spine.

The preschooler pointed behind her. Zack stepped out from behind the pine tree in the front yard. Maddie gasped, and then her feet were in motion before her brain caught up. She pounded down the stairs, across the grass, and threw herself into Zack's arms. He easily caught her and swung her in a circle before lowering her onto her feet and giving her a kiss for the memory books.

"And to think he was worried how you might react to seeing him," Brooks said drily from behind them.

Maddie broke away from Zack's kiss and stared up into his handsome face. "I was going to track you down."

"You were?" He quirked an eyebrow, rubbing his thumb along her cheek before stealing another quick kiss.

Maddie giggled. "I've been researching boats to charter. My friend, Abby, and I were going to sail the Caribbean until we could invade your island."

Zack chuckled, and she felt it against her own chest. "I'm glad we came. It might've taken you months to find me."

Months? She couldn't have handled that. "I'm glad you came too." More than she could express, especially with Brooks watching them with a wry grin on his face and Chalise tugging on Zack's shirt.

"Uncle Zack? Is this my new friend Maddie?"

Maddie bent down and gave the little girl a hug. "I am, sweetheart." She glanced up at Zack with the question in her eyes.

Zack picked up the little girl and Maddie straightened to face them. "My parents gave me custody of Chalise after she started speaking to me."

Maddie gasped and placed her hand over her lips. "That's wonderful, Zack."

"And Chalise and I have a proposition for you. We worked out a little compromise with my father, spending time in New York and the island."

"Wait. You're working for him?" Maddie's mind whirled. Zack's father was still putting conditions on him, but Zack seemed okay with it. What was Zack and Chalise's proposition? He'd included the information about New York and the island in the same breath. Did he want her to come with them? They didn't know each other well enough to decide to be together, but the thought of being apart from him was horrid.

"Yes." Zack set Chalise down. "Can you go with Brooks and get the car?" he asked his niece.

Brooks rolled his eyes. "Come on, love, they need their privacy. If you reject his offer, you can come to Cozumel with me," he called to Maddie.

"If only you were so lucky."

"Someday, you'll want a slice of this," Brooks returned.

"Maybe in the next life," Maddie teased him, but she couldn't take her eyes off Zack.

"Ouch, that's a long time to wait." Brooks and Chalise walked hand in hand to a Lexus parked a couple of houses down.

"I have a proposal for you." Zack pressed his hands together and shifted his weight.

Maddie liked that he was nervous, because she felt the same. She pulled the side of her lip between her teeth and waited, but he didn't continue. She nodded to him. "Yes?"

Zack chuckled uneasily. "Sorry. I just want you to say yes, so I've been struggling for the past couple of hours deciding how to phrase it best."

He looked so cute when he was uncertain like this. "I can't promise I'll say yes, but I won't beat you up for phrasing it wrong." Maddie's heart thumped uncontrollably. When he said propose, did he mean *propose*? She couldn't say yes to *that* right now, but maybe if they got to know each other better—and oh, how she wanted to get to know him better.

"Good point." He rubbed a hand over his bald head. "What would you think of coming with me to New York and then back to the island and being Chalise's nanny?"

Maddie blinked at him. She had a master's degree and he wanted her to be a nanny?

"You're completely overqualified, I know that, but I want to be with you, to get to know you, and who better to work with and teach Chalise than someone with your expertise? I'll pay you double, triple, what you were going to make in your job, and I'll cover all your expenses."

Maddie's jaw dropped open. The money didn't matter to her, considering what her father had given her. She wanted the chance to help children, but she wanted the chance to be with Zack, too. She took a long breath as he watched her, his eyes filled with a plea. The longer she waited, the more his dark eyes dimmed.

Maddie pursed her lips and tilted her head to the side. "How long is this shindig?"

"Until you're sick of us."

Maddie wanted to tell him she'd never get sick of him, but she didn't know that. She did know she wanted to get to know him and be with that darling little girl. An idea came that would allow her to help other children like she'd dreamed. She swallowed and said, "I have a few requests."

Zack pushed out a loud breath and took a step closer to her. "Name them," he whispered in a husky voice that made her tremble.

"When we're in New York, I want to find a way to work with underprivileged children with speech difficulties. And when we're at the island, I want to do the same thing in Belize a few days a month."

Zack grinned. "I thought you were going to have a hard request."

"What would a hard request be?"

"No kissing or something like that."

Maddie laughed. "That would be a crazy idea."

Zack trailed a hand up her arm along her shoulder and to her neck. He gently pulled her closer to him. "Would it?"

Maddie licked her lips and stared up at his handsome face. She wrapped her arms around his strong back. "It would be insane."

Zack lowered his head. His breath brushed her mouth, warm and tinged with peppermint. "Let's agree to lots of kissing."

"I'm in."

Zack grinned and covered the distance to her mouth. His kiss was warm and full of desire and promise. Maddie savored each moment of his touch and knew she'd made the right decision.

CHAPTER SIXTEEN

Several months had passed, and Maddie couldn't say every day was perfect, but it was the best time she'd ever had in her life. She was head over heels in love with Chalise and even more so with Zack. They'd spent time in New York, Montana, Belize, toured Europe when Zack had work there, and—best of all—his island.

Maddie glanced around at the beautiful pool and gardens, palm trees, the beach, and the ocean beyond.

Chalise came running into the great room from her bedroom. "Auntie Maddie, when is Uncle Zack going to be back?"

"Hopefully soon, love." Zack had run to Belize for a few supplies. They usually went with him, but he'd been insistent that he would be quick and needed to go alone. It was so off for him to not want them to come with him that Maddie didn't argue, though Chalise wasn't happy to be left behind. She wanted to visit her best friend, Isabella, at the Start of Life Orphanage. Isabella was three years old and absolutely gorgeous with her short dark hair in tight cornrows. They all loved her and her chubby little brother, Alex.

"Shall we read while we wait for him?" She'd tried to keep Chalise busy all day with preschool sheets and a painting project. After lunch they'd played in the ocean and sand and swam in the pool. They should probably start dinner, but it wasn't much fun without Zack around to help her cook.

"Okay, but I wish Uncle Zack would hurry." Chalise stuck out her lower lip in a pout so cute Maddie couldn't help but laugh.

"Me, too."

Chalise cuddled into her arms, and Maddie grabbed a Junie B. Jones book. A little humor would be good for both of them right now. She was into the third chapter when suddenly Chalise screamed, "The boat! Uncle Zack's coming!"

Chalise scrambled off her lap and dashed out the patio door. Maddie kept pace with the little girl as they ran down the stairs to the dock and along to the yacht. Maddie's face was split in a grin bigger than Chalise's. Zack was coming. The boat sailed into the harbor, and Maddie could see Zack's bald head and handsome face. He was really here. It was pathetic how much she missed him when he'd only left early that morning.

He came out and tossed the lines over. Maddie went to grab one, but stopped when a small dark head appeared at Zack's knee.

"Uncle Zack!" Chalise called happily to him. Then her mouth dropped open. "Izzy! You came to my house to play?"

Isabella giggled. "I'm gonna be your sista!"

"Yay!" Chalise cheered, jumping in the air.

Isabella popped off the yacht and hugged Chalise, then went into Maddie's open arms. Zack tied the boat off and came to her side. He wrapped his arms around Maddie and gave her a quick kiss on the lips. "I missed you."

"You have no idea how much we've missed you."

"We or you?"

"Both, but mostly me." She kissed him longer.

Isabella squirmed from Maddie's arms. "I wanna see my new house."

Chalise took her hand, and the two girls bounced up the dock and onto the stairs. Maddie and Zack followed, his arm around her waist. She worried that Isabella was going to be disappointed when she had to go back to the orphanage. Should she correct her now or let her enjoy her stay? Heaven knows the little angel hadn't been away from the orphanage very often.

"Oh, the supplies." Maddie stopped.

"I'll get them in a minute."

"You got me Dr. Pepper?" she asked.

"I'd never dare forget that."

Maddie grinned. He took such good care of her. "How did you talk them into letting you bring Isabella for a visit?"

They'd been begging the director of the orphanage for the past month to let them bring Isabella here. Maddie secretly wished they could adopt her, but she wanted to be married to Zack first. Her face heated up. She was about ready to propose. Being with Zack and Chalise was all she wanted now, and the opportunities Zack had created for her and Chalise to help children were everything she'd dreamed of.

"Well ..." They stopped at the top of the stairs, where Chalise was showing Isabella the pool toys.

"Can we swim?" Chalise asked.

"After dinner," Zack said. "Can you go show Izzy your room?"

"Can we share my room?" Chalise clasped Izzy's hand tighter, and they both jumped up and down and squealed.

"Sure."

The girls streaked into the house.

Maddie put her hand on Zack's shoulder. "You shouldn't let them get their hopes up. It'll just hurt more when they find out Izzy has to go back."

Zack turned to Maddie. He trailed his hand along her cheek. "They agreed that we could adopt Izzy."

"Seriously? Oh, Zack, thank you." Maddie's heart leapt into her throat. She loved Izzy so much.

"On one condition." Zack grinned and dropped onto one knee. He pulled out a ring box and flipped it open. A huge round diamond was set in a wide gold band.

Maddie gasped and put a hand over her mouth.

"We have to be married."

"*Have* to be?" Maddie tossed her hair, narrowing her eyes at him.

"What kind of a crappy proposal is that?"

Zack chuckled and reached for her hand. "Maddie, I want to marry you more than I've ever wanted anything. I figured if I brought Izzy along, you wouldn't say no."

Maddie tugged on his hand, and he stood. She kissed him for several wonderful minutes, then pulled back. "I would've married you without Izzy, but it's the best wedding present in the world."

Zack cupped her face with his hands. "There is one other small condition."

"Oh no, here it comes." Maddie couldn't stop smiling.

"We have to take Izzy back tomorrow and get married before they'll let us make it official."

"So I have one day to plan a wedding?"

Zack ducked his head. "Yeah, sorry. I know it's every girl's dream to plan a big wedding."

"Not mine. I do wish your parents, my mom, Brooks, and Abby could be here." She'd spent several different weeks with his parents and really grown to love his mom. His dad was trying in his own way, and his and Zack's relationship was slowly improving.

"They're all on their way."

"A little overconfident that I'd say yes?" Maddie grinned and covered his hand with hers.

"I've been a wreck all day worrying." He winked. "Are you really okay without a big wedding?"

"Yes. I just want you, Chalise, Izzy ... oh, and I really want Alex." Isabella's baby brother was almost six months old now, all chub and smiles. Maddie ached for that little boy when they weren't with him.

Zack pulled the ring out of the box and gently slid it on her finger. "You're amazing, Madeline Panetto. It's already worked out. We pick Alex and Izzy up right after the honeymoon."

Maddie screamed, then kissed him again. "I love you!"

"I love you, too." He simply held her close, then leaned back and smiled. "We're starting out with three children; do you think it's a stretch to get to eight?"

Maddie giggled. He was going to be the best dad, and she was so blessed to be with him. "I think we should have four or five of our own, then adopt as many as they'll let us."

Zack trailed his hands through her hair. "My dad is going to have a fit when I'm too busy with babies to work like he wants."

"He can deal with you working less. I'm the boss around here."

Zack laughed. "That you are, my love. That you are." He kissed her until the girls came demanding food.

Zack gave them each a cheese stick to tide them over and sat them at the bar. He and Maddie held hands, and he turned to her. "Do you want to give them the news?"

Maddie wiped at her eyes, suddenly overcome with the emotion of it all. "Chalise, Izzy. What do you think if you both start calling us Mom and Dad and we are all a family?"

The girls squealed with delight and hugged each other. Maddie wished she had a picture of it. They were so cute.

"We're also going to go get Alex, and he'll be part of our family too."

"I get a little brother?" Chalise yelled. "Yippee!"

"And we're going to buy you both beautiful dresses tomorrow so Maddie and I can get married," Zack said.

"Can we eat at a restaurant after?" Isabella asked. They'd taken her away from the orphanage to eat a few times, and she was obsessed with it.

"The nicest restaurant I can find," Zack assured her.

"Thank you, Daddy." Isabella beamed up at him.

Daddy. Maddie loved that her little girls would have the most loving, fun, and protective daddy ever. Zack hurried around the bar to hug Isabella. Chalise went into his other arm. Maddie walked to all of them, and they formed a circle with the girls between their arms.

"This is the best family ever!" Chalise declared.

Maddie smiled at Zack over the girls' heads. "I completely agree."

ABOUT THE AUTHOR

Cami is a part-time author, part-time exercise consultant, part-time housekeeper, full-time wife, and overtime mother of four adorable boys. Sleep and relaxation are fond memories. She's never been happier.

Sign up for Cami's newsletter to receive a free ebook copy of *The Feisty One: A Billionaire Bride Pact Romance* and information about new releases, discounts, and promotions here.

If you enjoyed *Caribbean Rescue,* please keep reading for an excerpt of Zack's hilarious friend Brooks' story in Cozumel Escape.

www.camichecketts.com
cami@camichecketts.com

EXCERPT FROM COZUMEL ESCAPE

Brooks Hoffman whistled as he walked along the touristy marketplace of Cozumel. It was a beautiful eighty degrees with a slight breeze coming off the ocean, and since there wasn't a cruise ship in town today, the market was a bit quieter than usual. That meant fewer women, but there were sacrifices he was willing to make for a peaceful shopping trip before Christmas.

He'd already found toys for Zack and Maddie's three children, but he wanted to find something pretty for Maddie, and he had no clue what to buy Zack. His closest friend was taking his family to New York for the holidays to be with his parents. If Brooks wanted to give them presents, he'd have to be ready when he went to visit them on their island for Thanksgiving weekend.

A gorgeous, pint-sized blonde breezed in front of him, tossing him an intriguing smile, her blue eyes sparkling. She ducked into a women's clothing shop before he could turn on the charm.

What was that little dream doing on his island? No cruise ships in port meant she was staying for a week or beyond. Dare he hope she was here for longer than a week? He tsked at himself. He'd never dated any woman longer than a week, so what did it matter? His grin grew.

This one was intriguing enough that it might take longer than a week to tire of her.

He followed her light scent into the women's shop. Apparently, this was the place Maddie would receive her Christmas present from this year.

"Can I help you?" the young attendant called out while folding a cobalt-blue shirt. She glanced up and smiled at him. "Ah. Señor Hoffman. So good to see you, sir."

"You as well." Most of the island knew Brooks by name. He hired a lot of locals, and they'd become his close friends. What could he say? This was his kingdom. Of course they revered him.

He glanced around for the woman. She was in the back, sifting through long dresses on a rack. He sidled his way up to her, bent down, and murmured, "The blue would match your eyes beautifully."

She jumped and took a swing at him.

Brooks stepped back quickly to avoid getting smacked by the woman. She was so small he could bench-press her without raising his heart rate, but her punch had been quick and sure.

"Oh, sorry!" Her cheeks reddened. *How intriguing, a woman that blushed easily.* "I didn't hear you approach, and all of a sudden you're, like, whispering in my ear."

Brooks arched an eyebrow. He liked the way she talked—blunt, and with a Southern accent that could drive a man to buy unnecessary jewelry.

"How in the world did you sneak up on me? You're stinking huge!"

"Training." He was never going to elaborate. "So, South Carolina? Maybe Georgia?"

"Alabama."

"Ah. I like it. Here for a week, or can I persuade you to stay longer?" He winked, and she blushed again. *Ah, innocence.* It could never be bested in his opinion.

"I live here." Her lips turned down and she brushed by him. "If you'll excuse me."

Brooks reached out and gently gripped her arm. She glared down at his fingers, then up at him. How could a woman this interesting live here and he not know about it?

"I don't know if I can excuse you." He took his voice to the depth he knew drove women crazy. "I haven't seen eyes that brilliantly blue in years and find myself quite drawn to you. Dinner tonight?"

"No, but thanks all the same for the invite," she said, with just the right amount of sauce in her voice, like Southern barbecue—sweet and tangy.

"You can thank me later," he murmured.

Those blue eyes snapped up at him, and her pretty pink lips puckered as if she'd licked the salt off of a margarita. Hmm. Salt, margaritas, and her lips. He liked it.

She tugged her arm back, and he released her because he was a gentleman first and foremost. As a child, he'd seen too many men take advantage of women. That would never be him.

She speed walked to the front of the shop. Luckily for both of them, he was quick as a panther. "At least tell me where you're staying. If you're lucky enough, I could convince you to have drinks with me."

She whirled, and her eyes went up his body, down, and up again. Brooks flexed his arms slightly, certain she would like what she saw. A man doesn't spend hours in the gym every day for his health.

Tilting her head to the side, she let that luscious blonde hair spill over her toned and tanned shoulder. He looked forward to an opportunity to pick her up and kiss her until she begged for more. Ah. His life was good.

"I don't drink."

"Oh? Dinner then." He dusted his hands off. It was settled. "When and where shall I pick you up?"

She took a step closer to him, and he couldn't hide a smile of triumph. She'd come around quickly. They always did.

"You can come have dinner with us. I believe our cook is whipping up somethin' special tonight." That accent was being applied thick as frosting. "Tortillas and beans."

Tortillas and beans? Was she kidding? Any child on the island could make tortillas and beans. "Hmm? Yes, while that does sound appetizing ..." She was appetizing, but her dinner offer definitely was not. Yet, it was an opportunity to spend time with her. Sometimes good food had to be sacrificed to woo said lady. "Where is this dinner to be held?"

"Bethel Orphanage. You might've heard of it, just a half mile inland from here." She whirled and stomped from the store.

Brooks's jaw unhinged. Sheer terror rushed through him at the idea of setting foot in the building. The orphanage? He donated vast amounts of money to that orphanage, but had never made it past the wooden front door. The memories of hunger and pain would crash around him, and someone might find out that the mighty Brooks Hoffman was simply a scared little boy who had buried his past rather than deal with it.

"Are you going to go?" The smooth-skinned shopkeeper was by his side.

Brooks pasted his confident smile back on. "Ah, no. I've had enough tortillas and beans to last me a lifetime." He threw his shoulders back and strutted out of the shop before she asked any more questions.

***

I hope you enjoyed the first chapter of Brook's story. To continue reading click here.

EXCERPT FROM SHADOWS IN THE CURTAIN

EMMALINE PRETENDED SHE DIDN'T FEEL his eyes on her as she strode to the leg press. It didn't matter where she was in the gym; he discreetly watched. She was flattered, but married. Although a beautiful distraction, she couldn't allow herself to be taken in by him.

She should've done one more set of rows, but she had to get out of there—get away from those blue eyes and back to the reality of the man she loved, the man she'd pledged her life to.

Emmy grabbed her keys and jacket from the shelves by the door and reached for the handle, mumbling a thank-you to the attendant. The door burst open from the outside; two teenagers scurried through. Emmy was knocked to the side and lost her balance. A pair of strong arms wrapped around her from behind, catching her. She found her footing, whirled in the man's embrace, and looked into pools of blue, sparkling like the ocean in Tahiti.

Her mouth hung open. Besides their exchange after *Joseph* several weeks ago, she'd kept her distance. She'd forced herself to forget those eyes with brown lashes longer than any woman's, the strong jawline and slightly hollowed cheeks that had dimples in them when he smiled —which he was doing right now.

"Are you okay, sweetheart?"

Her lips compressed. She was nobody's sweetheart but Grayson's. Emmy pulled free of his grasp. Risking one more glance into those eyes, she realized she needed to wipe the dimples from his face before she tripped on purpose so he'd catch her again. "Tell me you have a beautiful wife and at least two adorable children at home and you're just smiling at me because you're an incredibly nice guy who has no agenda where I'm concerned."

Dimples erased. He exhaled slowly, eyes darkening like a storm blowing in. "No wife and no adorable children."

Emmy folded her arms across her chest. To his credit, his eyes didn't rove from hers, but when she thought about it, they never did. Every time she caught his gaze on her, he was looking at her face, not her body.

"Yeah, well, I do," she said. "Awesome husband, that is, and he wouldn't appreciate the way you're always checking me out."

He didn't look away, nor did he deny it. He brushed a hand through his longish sandy-blond hair before nodding slowly. "You're right. I, um, never noticed a ring or had the guts to talk to you before now. Now that I know you're married ..." He swallowed. "... I won't bother you again."

Something inside her melted at the sad look in his eyes and his admission that he hadn't dared approach her and wouldn't have even been looking if she'd worn her ring. It was just obnoxiously huge and rubbed against her finger when she lifted weights. She'd buy a gold band today.

"Thanks." For some reason, she wanted to reassure him, maybe bring back one of the dimples. She forced a smile. "No worries for you, since every other woman in Cannon Beach is after you." Did that sound as awkward to him as it did to her?

He frowned and held the door open for her. She nodded to him before slinking through the door and could've sworn he said, "But not the right woman."

Waves softly crashed on the beach a hundred feet from their home.

Emmy leaned on the deck railing, soaking up the new day, the salt in the air, her wet hair dampening her shirt, and the sun warming her forehead. She only had fifteen minutes to dry her dark hair, put some makeup on, and eat breakfast before her first voice student showed up, but she wanted to sit and watch the ocean, go on a walk, or better yet, take a long swim.

Grayson came up behind her, resting his chin on top of her head. She smiled at the feel of his tall, gangly body wrapped around her. He was so comfortable to lean against. They'd spent their teenage years as neighbors and best friends. Grayson had pursued her for years before she agreed to marry him. Then he'd moved her away from the craziness of L.A. and the theater crowd who would trample anyone to be on top. Now she acted at a lesser theater with people she adored, taught music to sweet children, and loved every minute with her husband. With the exception of the disturbing notes, the past year had been the most content and peaceful time of her life.

"You want to go swimming?" he guessed.

She sighed. "Yes, but I've got a student coming any minute and I'm sure you have a lot of work to do."

He kissed her hair. "I'll watch you when I get home." He'd opened a branch of his software company in Portland and enjoyed driving into work on occasion, but he ended up flying to his main facility in L.A. at least twice a week. He was gone more than she liked, but he took his success and his products very seriously.

"Thanks," she said. "That would be great."

Grayson assumed she would give up swimming in the ocean when they'd moved to the cooler waters of Oregon. She argued that with a full-length wetsuit, she was as warm as she'd been in California. He'd finally played the petrified husband card and made her swear to only swim if he came with her or watched from the beach. She didn't doubt his love, but sometimes she felt smothered. Her acting career was just like her swimming. He had come to every practice and performance he could since the threatening notes began. If he realized men were hitting on her at the gym, he'd get a membership tomorrow.

He pressed a soft kiss to her lips. As always, Emmy hoped for passion to ignite within her at his kiss. As always, it was pleasant and short.

She glanced back at the beach and saw the man from the gym. Swallowing, she forced herself not to react. *What is he doing here?* He met her gaze.

She drew a couple of shaky breaths before turning and focusing on her husband.

The ringing phone gave her an excuse to go inside.

"Drive safe," Emmy said to Grayson as she walked into their two-story living room and reached for the cordless on the coffee table.

"Love you." Grayson closed the sliding glass door and then left through the garage entrance off the laundry room.

"Love you too." She pushed the button on the phone. "Hello."

"Emmaline," Aunt Jalina's voice screeched in her ear. "I read some wonderful reviews about your performance in *Joseph*. I'd be proud if you were actually performing with a company worth being called a company."

"Good morning, Auntie." Emmy shook her head. Aunt Jalina sounded in good spirits.

"It's an awful morning. When are you going to come home, or at least make that skinny husband of yours move you to Portland so you can perform with a respectable group?"

"And give up this view?" Emmy paused and smiled at the truth of her statement. Two-story windows showcased waves crashing on the beach. Haystack Rock decorated the background. "Not a chance. How's Uncle Carl?"

"Happy as ever—sends you his love."

Emmy smiled. At least she knew that her uncle loved her. Her aunt did in her own twisted way, but sometimes it was hard to feel through the criticism. "Give him a kiss for me. I've got to run; students are on their way."

"Students? You waste your abilities teaching children who could never rise to the talent and training you've been blessed with."

Emmy walked into the kitchen and put some bread in the toaster. "Oh, I don't know about that. I've got some very promising children here."

"Pshaw. You may think it's fun to tease me, Emmaline, but your mother would be rolling over in her grave."

Emmy clutched the butter knife in her hand. "Now that's where you're wrong, Auntie. My mother was proud of me no matter what."

"Your mother was proud because you were a success! What are you now? A twenty-five-year-old who's already washed up and given up."

Emmy stood to her full five feet six inches. She knew all her mother would've wanted was her happiness. "I am successful at what I'm doing. I'm happy and respected here. I'd never go back to that cesspool of cutthroats."

Jalina clucked her tongue. "Darling, I know you didn't enjoy L.A. I'm not saying you have to move back here, but please consider auditioning in Portland at least."

"Did I not speak clearly? I am happy here."

"Don't you get uppity with me! If you don't do something with your life ..." She paused, then continued with her shrill voice. "I will cut you out of my inheritance."

Emmy laughed at that. Jalina had no clue how wealthy Grayson was and how little Emmy cared for the money. "Oh, Auntie, when has money ever been a motivator for me?"

"It should be! You know how horrible it is to go without."

Emmy's young life had been filled with want as her mother earned just enough to survive. Somehow there had always been money for Emmy's acting, vocal, and piano lessons. She'd been too young and loved the lessons too much to question why they didn't have enough food but could afford the best private tutors. "Don't pretend you don't feel guilty about that," Emmy said.

"If your mother wouldn't have lied to us all those years. She would only let me pay for your lessons. I had no clue."

She didn't go on, and Emmy was grateful. Her aunt and uncle were devastated when they'd finally forced her mother to let them visit her dilapidated Detroit apartment. They saw for themselves that Emmy's mother could barely afford rent and food, living off a waitress's salary after Emmy's father deserted them. Uncle Carl and Aunt Jalina moved them to Glendora, California, and spoiled them both until her mother died three years ago from the cancer that ate away her breasts and then her vital organs. Even though she'd been twenty-one, Emmy hadn't been prepared to lose her mom. She missed her mother's quiet and unfailing love.

Her aunt insisted Emmy finish her M.F.A. from American Conservatory Theater in San Francisco before auditioning with the best companies in L.A. At twenty-four she had been an acclaimed performer, but miserable. She had no hope of rescue until Grayson talked her into marrying him and moved her away from it all.

A loud rap came from the sliding glass door.

"I've got a student here, Auntie." Emmy hung up without waiting for goodbye and motioned to her next-door neighbor to come in. "Student" was a loose term to use—she considered Kelton and his family her closest friends.

Kelton's white teeth split his copper skin as he thrust the back door open. "How's the prettiest voice teacher in Cannon Beach?"

"*Only* voice teacher in Cannon Beach." Emmy rolled her eyes. "I'll be better when I hear you practiced every day this week."

"Ha. We both know I only take lessons so I can come visit you and keep my momma from kicking me in the butt." The brawny defender for Seaside High's lacrosse team made it clear that hitting the gym and flirting with girls were more important than developing his musical ability.

Emmy shook her head, hiding a smile at his usual antics. The boy was inappropriate, but she loved him like the nephew she'd never had. "We're both going to kick your behind if you don't start practicing."

Kelton shrugged innocently and made his way to the piano. Emmy forgot about missing breakfast, her aunt, and the man from the gym as she played the piano and encouraged her uncommitted yet talented neighbor.

***

I hope you enjoyed this excerpt from *Shadows in the Curtain*. To continue reading click here.

ADDITIONAL WORKS

by Cami Checketts

Dying to Run

Running Home

Full Court Devotion: Christmas in Snow Valley

A Touch of Love: Summer in Snow Valley

Running from the Cowboy: Spring in Snow Valley

Light in Your Eyes: Winter in Snow Valley

Christmas Makeover: Echo Ridge Romance

The Fourth of July

Poison Me

The Colony

Made in the USA
Columbia, SC
05 August 2023

21295707R00091